A King Product

A Novel

JOY DEJA KING

ISBN 13: 978-1942217435
ISBN 10: 1-942217-43-9
Cover concept by Joy Deja King
Cover Model: Joy Deja King
Library of Congress Cataloging-in-Publication Data;
King, Deja Joy

Typesetting: Anita J.
Editor: Jacqueline Ruiz: tinx518@aol.com
Stackin' Paper Part 3: a novel/by Joy Deja King
For complete Library of Congress Copyright info visit;
www.joydejaking.com Twitter: @joydejaking

A King Production
P.O. Box 912, Collierville, TN 38027

This Book is Dedicated To My:

Family, Readers, and Supporters.
I LOVE you guys so much. Please believe that!!

—Joy Deja King

"We Were Beginners In The Hood As Five Percenters. But Something Must Have Got In Us, Cause All Of Us Turned To Sinners..."

—AZ

A KING PRODUCTION

Stackin'

PAPER
II
Born Sinners

A Novel

JOY DEJA KING

Chapter One

Like It Was Yesterday

Attorney Meissner read through the paperwork with meticulousness. The only sound made was when he turned a page. That level of silence was borderline haunting, but his thoroughness is what made Frank Meissner one of the most sought after criminal attorneys in the nation.

"Genesis, the federal government has built a pretty solid case against you."

"Fuck!" Genesis mumbled shaking his head

and looking down at his all orange attire in distress.

"I said a pretty solid case,"he stated raising his index finger.

"So what are you saying?"

"Pretty solid and full proof are two different things. That means there is wiggle room, how much wiggle room is the question. But I'll have that answer once I do some further investigating."

"How long will that take?"

"I have a fully staffed law office and half of them will be dedicated to working your case."

"I hope so with the retainer I paid you. But the late great Quentin Jacobs said you were the best criminal attorney money could buy. He made me promise that if I ever got in any legal trouble again, I would utilize your services."

"Quentin was not only one of my best clients, but he was also a dear friend. I'm sorry you weren't able to attend his funeral."

"I am too, but he knows I was there in spirit." Genesis put his head down for a moment thinking how horrible it must've been for him to die at the hands of his daughter. They all knew Maya was crazy, but no one ever guessed that she was capable of killing her own father.

"I'm sure he did. I promise you, Genesis,

you're in good hands. If I can't beat this case for you, nobody can."

"Does that mean you're recommending turning down the plea deal the Feds are offering?"

"Definitely! Let me do my job. If it comes down to a plea deal, we'll be the ones making it. Until then, hold tight. I know you're disappointed that the judge denied bail, but I'm working on some things," Mr. Meissner said gathering up his paperwork and putting it in his brief case. "I'll be in touch tomorrow, but of course call me if you need anything."

Genesis nodded his head as he was led back to his cell. He lay on his bunk, staring up at the ceiling, imagining he was anywhere else other than being locked behind prison walls. He had flashbacks to the last time he was facing doing double digits behind bars. Genesis then reflected back to when he was eleven years old and remanded to a juvenile detention center after killing his drug-addicted, abusive father.

He was only trying to protect his mother who was being beat to a pulp. After years of seeing his mother abused by his father, each time with her being on the brink of death, he snapped. That incident was so vivid to Genesis, as if it happened yesterday instead of over thirty years ago. Now here he was back in the very place he had wanted to escape, in a cage like an animal.

Life had not been kind to Genesis. He was dealt a bad hand. Part of him was tired of being in the jungle, struggling to survive in the streets. When the Feds came to arrest him, he had resigned himself to spending the rest of his life behind bars. All that changed the day Supreme came to visit him. He now had a reason to fight for his freedom. His wife was alive and Genesis wouldn't stop until he was reunited with Talisa.

"We're gonna have to clear out of here soon." Julio stood up angrily. "There has been no contact from Arnez in months. This island is far from a paradise if we have no money to maintain it."

"What about the number of that guy Arnez gave you. Have you tried calling him?" Mario asked.

"You mean Markell?"

"Yeah...yeah. Him."

"I tried calling him too. I even called him yesterday and the number is now disconnected. I don't know what the hell is going on, but we can't continue to stay here without any money coming in. Soon all the staff is going to leave. Gabe already up and quit."

"I heard he hit the lottery," Mario commented.

"I'm glad you can make jokes under these circumstances."

"I'm not joking. That's what he telling people. I have family that live near him. They say he got a new sports car, lots of jewelry, and has been flashing money around," Mario said in a heavy Spanish accent.

"Really?" Julio looked at Mario with a raised eyebrow full of curiosity. "How did Gabe come into all this money? Did he really win the lottery, is that why he quit?"

"No! I don't believe that."

"But you have your own ideas as to how he came into all this money?" Julio inquired.

"I do." Mario nodded. "I think it has to do with that woman that miraculously disappeared off the island a few days before Gabe quit. I don't think that was a coincidence."

"Hmmm." Julio rubbed his chin in deep thought." No one had been paid in weeks and Gabe was desperate for money. He probably struck a deal with that woman."

"My thoughts exactly." Mario agreed.

"You might be right. Arnez mentioned she

had a very wealthy man in the states. He probably paid for her safe return. Gabe made off with who knows how much money and didn't even cut us in." Julio shook his head in disgust. "How dare he."

"So what are we gonna do about it?" Mario wanted to know.

"One woman is gone, but we have one left. Let's see how much we can get for her return," Julio suggested.

"But where would we start. We don't know how to get in contact with anyone that might be looking for this Talisa woman. And she's been on this island so long, she wouldn't have any contact information," Mario reasoned.

"You're right, but Gabe would. Arnez never told me how, but he mentioned the women were connected. So we'll start with whoever this person was that paid for Skylar's return. Gabe had to make contact with them to get the money. He will tell us who that person is or he will die," Julio said matter-of-factly.

Chapter Two

Whatever It Takes

"You looking a little stressed over there," Lorenzo said when he walked into Genesis's office and saw Amir behind the desk.

"Little isn't an accurate description. More like overwhelmingly stressed. Quentin is dead, Nico is in Miami, you're in LA and of course my dad is locked up. There's nobody to handle business but me. I thought I knew what I was doing, but the numbers are telling me something different."

Amir exhaled, leaning back in his chair.

"Don't be so down on yourself, Amir. This is too much for any one person to handle that's why there are multiple partners. The situation with your father and Quentin came out of nowhere and hit all of us hard. Nico was hoping to be back in New York by now, but he'll be staying in Miami for much longer than he expected. So that means you're stuck with me." Lorenzo shrugged.

"Wait! Are you saying that you're going to stay in New York to run the business with me?"

"Yep. That's what I'm saying. I've made all the necessary arrangements and I'll be here for however long you need me."

"Lorenzo, thank you man." Amir walked from around the desk to shake Lorenzo's hand. "You're a lifesaver. I didn't want to say anything, but I felt like I was drowning."

"Listen, I'm a partner in this business. It's not even fair for you to be doing this alone. I commend you for holding it down this long."

"That means a lot coming from you. My dad always speaks so highly of you and how you conduct business. I know you have a life in LA so coming here can't be easy."

"I'll make it work. My main concern was Dior, but she'll be here next week. So it's all good.

I wanted to be here anyway. Not just for business, but for your father. Genesis is in for the fight of his life. He needs all of our support."

"You're right. He'll be glad to know you're here."

"I'ma see him tomorrow. I want to reassure him that we'll be holding things down until he gets out."

"So you think he's gonna get out?" Amir questioned. "Tell me the truth."

"You're too grown for me to lie to you and too smart," Lorenzo stated, taking a seat. "Listen, I've been where your father is. It ain't nothing nice. There's always a chance when you in the game that you might have to sit down and do a long bid. Some are lucky, but most aren't. I'm not sure which one your father will be. What I do know is we're gonna do everything in our power to bring him home. Even if that means getting down in the gutter to do so."

Skylar was halfway asleep when she thought she heard a knock at the door. She shifted her body in bed finding a comfortable position, but the knocking was persistent. After another few minutes with the banging becoming louder, Skylar had to accept her afternoon nap wasn't meant to be. With reluctance she got out of bed, threw on her bathrobe and went to open the front door.

"Supreme, what are you doing here?" He was the last person Skylar was expecting to see on a Wednesday afternoon.

"I apologize for intruding, but I need to speak with you."

"I was actually taking a nap," Skylar said rubbing her eyes. "Can this wait? I haven't been able to sleep much since; you know Genesis was…" her voice faded off as if she didn't want to say the words.

"I'm here about Genesis."

"Is he okay…did something else happen?" Skylar's voice became panicked.

"Genesis is fine," Supreme said not wanting to upset her. "I just need to ask you a couple of questions. It shouldn't take that long and then you can get back to taking your nap."

"Sure, come in." Skylar tightened her bathrobe and sat down on the living room couch. "Can I get you anything to drink?" she offered.

"No, thank you, I'm fine. I know you wanna get back to bed so I'll get right to it," Supreme said sitting down across from Skylar. "I'm not sure if Genesis had an opportunity to tell you yet, but his wife Talisa is alive," Supreme stated not holding anything back.

Skylar coughed, patting her chest lightly trying to calm her nerves. It was either that or fall out on the floor from shock and fear knowing the secret she prayed would stay on that island was now out. Talisa was alive. "No, Genesis hasn't mentioned anything to me. Are you sure?"

"Positive."

"I see. So why are here talking to me?"

"Because the same man that kidnapped you also took Talisa all those years ago."

"I see. You're talking about Arnez?"

"Yes." Supreme nodded.

"I never saw Arnez."

"Well did you see Talisa?" Supreme's question was so blunt that at first Skylar hesitated to answer.

"If I had seen Talisa then I would've known she was alive, but I'm just finding this out. So to answer your question, no I never saw Talisa while I was on the island," she lied.

"I need you to think carefully. Do you remember where the island was?"

Skylar bit down on her bottom lip and stood

up, turning her back on Supreme. She didn't want him to see how nervous she was. "Like I told Genesis, I have no idea where the island was. They kept me blindfolded until I got there and I was blindfolded when they let me go."

"So you sure you don't remember anything that might help us locate Talisa?" Supreme pressed.

"No! If I did I would tell you," Skylar sniped becoming defensive. "Don't you think I would want to help bring Talisa home?"

"I wasn't trying to imply you wouldn't. I appreciate you taking the time to speak with me. I know this can't be easy for you."

"Why do you say that, Supreme? What!" Skylar's voice cracked. "Do you think the man I'm in love with and moved cross country to be near because I believed we were going to spend the rest of our lives together, is going to dump me now that he's found out his wife is alive? Is that why you say this can't be easy for me?" Skylar was no longer able to contain her emotions.

"I didn't mean to upset you, Skylar. I promised Genesis I would bring his wife home and I'm doing everything I can to keep that promise. I know you love Genesis and I know he loves you too..."

"But I'm not his wife," Skylar asserted cutting Supreme off. "I get it." Skylar regained her composure and wiped away the tears that had escaped her eyes. "Like I said I don't know anything. I'm sorry I can't be more helpful."

"Okay. Well if you remember anything you know how to get in touch with me."

"I do and I will," Skylar said walking Supreme out. Once she locked the door, she ran to the bathroom and began to vomit while crying simultaneously. Skylar didn't know which felt worse, the possibility of losing the man she loved to prison or to another woman.

Chapter Three

Next Move

Nichelle was lying on the beach with a Key Lime Plum Margarita in one hand and her iPhone in the other. As she enjoyed the perfect mixture of warmth beaming from the sun and the cool breeze brought by the ocean waves, Nichelle's heart dropped when she saw the headline from a newsfeed that popped up on her phone.

"We need to catch the next flight to New York," Nichelle turned to Renny and said. He was so engrossed reading Bloomberg Businessweek that he didn't even hear her. "Renny!" she shouted, determined to get his attention.

"Why you so loud?" Renny asked not looking up.

"Can you stop reading for one second and listen to me."

"Nichelle, you need to relax," he said finally making eye contact.

"The Feds arrested my brother. We have to go to New York. Now!" Nichelle insisted.

"I'll book the flights," Renny said without hesitation.

For the last few years, Nichelle had been living on the west coast, so she rarely saw Genesis, but they communicated frequently via text and email. Finding out that he had been arrested through a newsfeed on her phone made her furious. While Renny made the flight reservations she decided to call her nephew.

"Hey, Nichelle," Amir answered. Although Nichelle was his aunt because the age gap wasn't that wide and she was still pretty young, Amir always addressed Nichelle by her first name without the aunt in front.

"Why didn't you tell me your father was arrested?" Nichelle asked angrily.

"I was gonna call you, but my father told me not to. He didn't want you worrying. How did you find out?"

"It just popped up on my phone."

"I'm sorry you had to find out that way, Nichelle."

"How is he doing?"

"You know my dad. No matter what the situation is, he's gonna be a warrior."

"Well, Renny and I are on our way to New York. When I get there, I want to know everything that is going on with his case, including who's the attorney that's representing him. I refuse to let my brother spend the rest of his life behind bars. I'll call you when we get there," Nichelle said before ending the call.

"If we're gonna make this flight, we need to leave now," Rennyinformed his wife.

"Then we better go." Nichelle grabbed her tote bag and sprinted towards their car. She was resolute in her mission to get to New York and be with her brother. They had spent so many years apart and Nichelle refused to let Genesis face these criminal charges without being there to show her support.

"I did what you asked and met with your attorney," Lorenzo told Genesis as he sat down for his visitation.

"He didn't give you any problems did he? I told him you were coming to his office."

"No, he was straight. He let me read over all the information he received from the Feds so far. He even made me copies. I was up all last night reading over everything."

"Did anything stand out to you...something that my attorney might overlook?" Genesis questioned, knowing Lorenzo would follow what he was saying.

"At first glance nothing stood out. On the real, I still didn't notice the second go round, but the third time I caught it," Lorenzo nodded proudly.

"I knew if anyone would, it's you. You were always anal when going over our financial records." Genesis shook his head. "If one cent was off, you'd catch that shit." Both men laughed. "So tell me what you got."

"The informant isn't named. The identity is being kept anonymous for which isn't surprising. But another person that the Feds are investigating is mentioned, but not by name, only their initials. Clearly they're still building that case and figured by not using the full name it would be disregarded."

"That makes sense. My attorney would be more focused on the evidence against me not some other person they're investigating."

"Plus, your attorney would have no clue whose initials that could be. I mean I didn't even focus on it while I was reading, initially. Then I got to thinking. It couldn't be a coincidence that they're investigating you and this other person. There has to be a connection."

"But the only people I'm connected with in business is you, Nico, and Quentin who is no longer with us."

"That's another reason why I overlooked it because the initials weren't any of ours. It's D.B."

"D.B.," Genesis mouthed, frowning his face as he tried to figure out whom that could be. Having so many other conversations going on in the visitation room simultaneously did nothing to help with his focus. "Who the fuck is D.B." He began shaking his head becoming frustrated. Right when Lorenzo was about to help him out, Genesis blurted out, "Delondo Bryant."

"Bingo," Lorenzo stated. "Delondo has been

a heavy hitter for a long time."

"I haven't heard that nigga's name in a minute," Genesis said.

"Me neither. I know he's still in the game, but for the last few years he's tried to be real low key. Stay under the radar. The only reason why his name came to me is because the Feds mentioned a deal that went down in Philly. I remember you and Delondo were both handling business in Philly years ago at the same time. But whoever this informant is has to do business with both of you."

"Or we share the same enemy," Genesis shot back.

"What enemy do you and Delondo have in common?"

"Arnez Douglas. He shot Delondo and almost killed him. Arnez hates Delondo almost as much as he hates me."

"I had no idea. That makes sense, but isn't Arnez dead? He can't be the informant," Lorenzo reasoned.

"Supreme did tell me that Arnez was dead, but hell, we all thought he was dead before and we were wrong. But even if he was alive, I highly doubt Arnez would work with the Feds."

"But he would get someone else to do his

dirty work," Lorenzo countered.

"Exactly. We need to find out who that person is."

"I think we'll be able to figure that out once I track down Delondo. He's the key."

"I agree." Genesis nodded.

"The Feds' entire case is built around this informant. We take care of them, the case against you will disappear."

"So what's your next move?" Genesis was anxious to know.

"I'm already on it. I have someone tracking Delondo down. Once they make contact, I'll be making a trip to Philly," Lorenzo told him.

"Just be careful. Delondo is under investigation so that means he is being watched and his moves closely monitored. I don't need you added to this indictment," Genesis warned.

"Don't worry, I'll be careful. The Feds won't see me coming or going," Lorenzo stated confidently.

Chapter Four

This Is Not A Joke

"So baby, when we taking that trip to Antigua that you promised me?" Lacy licked her lips seductively, caressing Gabe's leg under the table at the restaurant where they were having dinner.

"Soon," he said smiling.

"You've been saying soon for the last month. What's the holdup?"

"I have to work a few things out."

"A few things like what...your wife? I thought

you said you all were separated."

"We are."

"Then why did my homegirl see you having lunch with her the other day. Hmmm?" Lacy said digging her nails into Gabe's upper thigh while giving him an evil smile.

"Lacy, baby calm down." Gabe was cringing in his chair, but trying not to make a scene. "We were discussing the divorce settlement. She knows that I've come into a lot of money and trying to shake me down. I'm trying to keep shit amicable so she doesn't take me to the cleaners. But the divorce is moving forward. You the only woman I wanna be with. You gotta believe me, baby," Gabe pleaded.

"You better be telling me the truth, Gabe," Lacy scoffed.

"I am. You my everything," he said, leaning over and kissing her. Lacy then eased up her grip on Gabe's thigh, releasing her claws. "How about we get outta here and go back to your place. You can put on that sexy negligee I bought you the other day."

"Sounds good. I'll even keep my heels on while we have sex. I know how much you like that," she teased biting down on his lip after they tongued each other down.

The two continued making out like teenagers as they exited the restaurant and headed to Gabe's car. The sex-crazed duo was so enthralled into each other that neither noticed they were being watched. Julio and Mario had been following Gabe, patiently waiting for the right moment to strike.

That opportunity presented itself when Gabe pulled into the driveway of Lacy's house. Instead of immediately opening the door and going inside, the two continued groping each other giving Mario and Julio ample time to park down the street and sneak up on the unsuspecting pair. They waited for Lacy to put her key in the door and unlock it. Once she did they attacked.

"Get inside, now!" Mario barked, shoving his gun in the back of Gabe's head as Julio did the same to Lacy.

"Please don't kill us. Here!" Lacy cried, trying to hand Julio her purse. "You can take all the money I have, just don't hurt me."

"I don't want yo' money!" Julio scoffed, shoving Lacy's purse out of his way. "Both of you sit down and don't say a word," he ordered. "Mario, lock the door," he said, keeping his gun on Gabe and Lacy.

In all of her hysteria, Lacy couldn't help but

notice how calm and quiet Gabe was being. She glanced at him with horror. "Did you set me up?!"

Gabe appeared to be mortified by her question. "No!"

"Didn't I tell you motherfuckers not to say a word!" Julio growled, shoving his gun in their faces.

"Julio man, why are you doing this?" Gabe asked, shaking his head in disbelief that the man he used to work for had a gun to his head.

"You know them?" Lacy mumbled.

"Yo, shut up!" Mario screamed at her, ready to knock the woman out. "This has nothing to do with you. But since you wit' this idiot, if he don't do right you'll suffer the consequences."

"What do you all want from me?" Gabe questioned, looking baffled.

"You've come into a lot of money." Julio chuckled. "How is it that someone with no job is all of a sudden so rich? Where did all this money come from? Inquiring minds want to know."

"He won the lottery!" Lacy uttered. Gabe glared at Lacy and his face tightened up, but he said no words.

"I hear that's what you been telling everyone," Mario said smiling. "So did you win the lottery?"

There was a long pause before Gabe

answered. "Yeah, I won the lottery."

Julio swung back his arm before striking Gabe in the jaw. Blood splattered out the side of his mouth as his two front teeth fell out. Lacy let out an ear-piercing scream before Mario quickly put his hand over her mouth.

"If you don't shut up, I'll break your neck," Mario warned. "Now shut the fuck up! Do you understand?" Lacy nodded her head with a swiftness.

"Gabe, are you positive that's the story you want to stick to? Because if you don't tell me the truth, the next blow will be to the head of your lady friend over there. Then we will take a ride to see your wife and we'll have some fun with her. You think you can come into all that money and not share. No, no, no."

"Okay...okay..." Gabe moaned, holding his mouth trying to stop the bleeding. "I didn't win the lottery. Skylar told me if I helped her escape from the island, her man would pay me a lot of money," he admitted.

Mario glanced over at Julio and gave him that I told you so look as both men smirked. "So who is her man?" Mario asked the question that both him and Julio wanted to know.

"Genesis. His name is Genesis Taylor. That's

who transferred the money into my account."

"For your sake you better have his contact information."

"I do. I still have his cell number. It's in my phone," Gabe said as the blood continued to gush from his mouth and down his chin.

"Where's your phone?" Julio asked.

"In my pocket."

Julio signaled for Mario to retrieve the cell. Once Gabe gave them the code to unlock the phone they went to the contacts and felt they hit gold when they found Genesis's information.

"You have what you came for. Can you leave now and let us be!" Lacy wailed.

"Sorry, can't do that," Julio said before busting one shot in Lacy's head and another in Gabe's. "Can't take the chance one of you going to the police." Julio shrugged.

"We got what we needed, we can go now," Mario said as he and Julio left out leaving the two dead bodies hunched over on the couch.

"It's good to see you," Amir said, giving Nichelle a hug. "When you said you were on the way, I didn't think you meant literally." Amir smiled.

"But I'm glad you did. It's nice to have some family support."

"I'm happy I can be here with you. This has to be hard. Not only for Genesis, but for you too."

"It is. It's always been my dad and me. Growing up without my mom, I think that made us even closer. Not having him around is hard." Amir sighed, his voice full of distress.

"What is his attorney saying? Do they have a strong case?"

"Honestly, I don't know. I spoke to my dad yesterday and he didn't go into much detail. He basically said the lawyer was on it. I do know that Lorenzo is working on some leads."

"Who is Lorenzo?"

"One of my dad's business partners. I don't think you ever met Lorenzo. But he's a good friend too. He's actually on the west coast too."

"Really?"

"Yeah, but he's gonna be staying in New York for awhile. You know, to help me run the business, with my dad being locked up and all."

"Where's Nico?"

"In Miami. He has some family business he's dealing with there. And you know Quentin is no longer with us."

"Yeah, I heard about that. I couldn't believe

it, especially when I found out he was killed by his own daughter. How tragic." Nichelle shook her head. "Poor Aaliyah, I'm sure she took that hard. I've been out the loop so long...are the two of you still together? I can never keep up. You all have a tendency of going back and forth." She laughed.

"Aaliyah is actually engaged to a guy named Dale."

"What!" Nichelle's eyes widened.

"Yeah. They're getting married in a few months."

"Seriously, how do you feel about that?"

"She's happy and I'm happy for her. I've moved on too."

"Is that right! Who's the lucky girl?"

"Justina." Amir grinned.

"You're back with Justina! Wow! I remember when you, Aaliyah, and Justina came to that concert together. You all were like the three musketeers, so young, sweet, and cute. Now you're running your father's business, Aaliyah is getting married, and you and Justina are back together."

"Yep, I guess the more things change the more they stay the same. Enough about my romantic life, how's married life for you?"

"Renny and I are good. Elijah is getting so big. It seems like yesterday he was just a baby. I still remember the first time I saw Tierra holding him. He's such a special child. When married life gets a little difficult, Elijah is always the one that brings me and Renny together."

"I know you love Elijah like he's your own, but I thought you and Renny would've had a baby together by now," Amir said. Nichelle turned away for a moment. "I'm sorry. Did I say something wrong, Nichelle?"

"No. It's just still a little hard for me to talk about it."

"I didn't mean to upset you."

"A couple years ago I did get pregnant, but I had a miscarriage," she revealed.

"I'm so sorry. I had no idea," Amir said, feeling bad he even brought up kids.

"Yeah, I didn't tell anybody, but Renny of course. I was so excited. I was only in my first trimester, but I had already planned out the next eighteen years of their life." Nichelle laughed, but that didn't hide the sadness in her voice. "I've been too afraid to try again. I don't think I could go through losing another baby. My heart wouldn't survive it."

"You have to do what's right for you. If you

ever decide you want to try again, you'll know it. But until then, don't rush it," Amir advised.

"I can't believe I'm having this discussion with my nephew." Nichelle smiled. "But believe it or not, talking to you about it has made me feel a lot better. I love Renny, but he isn't really good at emotional conversations."

"Men, we try to be so tough and strong. It can be difficult for us to show our emotions, especially when we don't know how to fix what's wrong."

"I get that. I mean…"

"Hold that thought for one second. That's my father's cell. I try not to miss any calls because more than likely it's about business," Amir said reaching for the phone.

"No problem, take your time," Nichelle said walking over to look at some pictures that were on the glass display cabinet.

"Hello," Amir answered.

"Mr. Taylor, how are you?"

"Good, how can I help you?"

"We have a mutual friend that you did some business with and I wanted to see if you would like to do some more…for a price that is," Julio stated hoping to spark the his interest which he did.

"Who is this and who is this mutual friend you speak of?" Amir questioned full of intrigue.

"Gabe. Does that ring a bell?"

"Yes, it does," Amir lied; not knowing who the hell the man was talking about, but curious to find out.

"Good. You paid a great deal of money to get back what Gabe had, I'm hoping you'll do the same for what I have."

"And what is it that you have?"

"A very beautiful woman by the name of Talisa. Does that name mean anything to you?"

"What sort of sick joke are you playing!" Amir yelled through the phone. The loudness of his voice startled Nichelle, as she turned to see what had Amir so upset.

"I'm assuming from the anger in your voice that the name Talisa means a lot to you. I can assure you this isn't a joke, Mr. Taylor. I have Talisa and if you want her back, you'll have to pay double what you paid to Gabe. I'll be in touch."

"Who the fuck...hello!" before Amir could finish his sentence he realized the caller hung up.

"Amir, who was that? What did they say that has you so upset?" Nichelle wanted to know.

"It's about my mother. The caller said he has my mother," Amir said in disbelief.

Chapter Five

Much Deeper

"How are you doing? I guess that's kind of a dumb question," Skylar said wishing she could reach over and touch Genesis, but that was against visitation policies.

"Under the circumstances, I'm doing okay. How about you? You look like you've lost weight."

"I've been a little stressed that's all."

"I made sure that you're financially straight. You're being provided for aren't you?"

"Yes, everything is good, but money can't replace you, Genesis. I miss you. I want you home with me and my son."

"How is my lil' man doing?"

"He's fine, but he keeps asking about you. He misses you almost as much as I do. I don't know how much longer I can tell him you're away on business."

"I hate that you have to lie to him." Genesis put his head down. That painful ache you get when you disappoint a child was one of the reasons he never wanted to get into a serious relationship with Skylar, but now it was too late.

"I wasn't trying to make you feel guilty."

"I know, but I do. Ever since you came into my life, I've brought you nothing but chaos."

"Genesis, I chose to come into your world. You warned me what could happen. I didn't step into this blindly. I'm with you because I want to be. My question is do you want me in your life?"

"Of course I do. Why would you even ask me that?"

"Supreme came to see me. He told me your wife is alive. Why did I have to find that out from him?" Skylar asked.

"I was gonna tell you. I'm sorry you had to find out from Supreme. He's trying to locate

Talisa for me. I guess maybe he thought you could be some help."

"When were you gonna tell me?"

"Honestly I don't know. Between being locked up and then finding out that my wife is alive, I have a lot on my mind."

"That's what you always wanted, to have your wife back. I guess I should be happy for you, but what does that mean for us?"

"Skylar, let's not do this...not now. I might be spending the rest of my life behind bars. Even when Supreme brings Talisa back, she'll be coming home to a husband that's in prison. So before any decisions are made let's just wait."

"I can't wait. I'm pregnant with your child, Genesis. I've been having morning sickness. That's why I'm losing weight.

Genesis shook his head in dismay. This was the last thing he wanted to hear. "Do you really want to have my baby? There's a very good chance that our child would grow up without a father. I don't want that for my child."

"You would want me to have an abortion?" Skylar asked with tears in her eyes.

"Would you rather bring my son or daughter to visit me here? You would want them to grow up knowing their father is in a cage like I'm an animal. What sort of life is that?" Genesis kept shaking his head in frustration at the severity of his current circumstances.

"I rather deal with that than living the rest of my life knowing I killed our baby."

"I'm not trying to hurt you, Skylar, but if by some miracle I can beat these charges and get out of jail, I plan on spending the rest of my life with Talisa."

"So what are you saying, you wouldn't want to be apart of our child's life?"

"Of course I'll be apart of our child's life. I will be the best father that I can be, but that's all I'll be...their father. There won't be an us."

"I'm glad we finally got that out the way," Skylar said with a stoned face. "I guess it took the baby news for you to keep all the way real with me."

"Bringing a child into the equation changes everything. It's only fair I put all the cards on the table. You're the one that has to carry this baby and give birth. You deserve to have all the facts before making your decision."

"The decision has been made, Genesis. I'm having our baby. If you want to live happily ever after with Talisa then so be it, but it doesn't change a damn thing for me. I think I've stayed long enough," Skylar said, standing up.

"Skylar wait!" Genesis reached out to take her hand.

"No touching!" the guard barked.

"Don't leave like this," Genesis pleaded pulling his hand away before the guard walked over.

"It's better that I go. I need to start getting used to not having you in my life."

Genesis was crushed as he watched Skylar walk out the room. He knew that he cared immensely for Skylar and even had love for her, but Genesis had to admit to himself that as much as he loved Talisa his feelings also ran deep for Skylar.

"Are you sure I can't come with you," Precious said as Supreme packed a large duffel bag.

"I wish you could, but this isn't a vacation, baby. It's business. I'm hoping to be back in a couple of days."

"Even when you're handling business you have to sleep. Wouldn't it be nice to come back to your hotel and have me in the bed waiting for you," Precious said sprinkling kisses on

Supreme's neck.

"Babe, don't make this harder than it has to be. You'll be nothing but a distraction."

"A good distraction," she continued taking the kisses from his neck to his chiseled chest.

"Don't do this. I'm already running late for my flight," Supreme said with his eyes closed trying to fight temptation. But that didn't stop Precious.

"You taste so good," Precious looked up and said after deep throating Supreme's rock hard dick. She then kissed the tip before taking it all back in her wet mouth.

"You know you ain't right," Supreme gave a deep sigh unable to resist her. He lifted Precious up taking off her lace lingerie. He cupped her breasts licking his tongue around her nipples. She moaned in pleasure ready to have all of Supreme inside of her.

"Making love to you always feels like the first time," Precious whispered in Supreme's ear before he entered her. Each thrust more powerful and passionate than the last. Precious wrapped her legs around his lower torso, placing her hands on his muscled buttocks pressing him deeper and deeper inside of her walls. Her cries of pleasure became louder until they both reached their climax. "That was perfect," she purred.

"Yes, it was and now all I want to do is lay inside of you, but I can't," Supreme breathed heavily, turning over on his back.

"You can always cancel your trip and stay here with me."

"I can't."

"What business are you going to handle that's so important?" Precious wanted to know.

"It's for Genesis."

"Genesis?!" Precious rose up in the bed. "When did you start doing business with Genesis?" She gave him a stunned side glance.

"Please don't ask me a million and one questions, but I found out that Genesis's wife is still alive."

"You're positive?"

"Yes. I went to visit Genesis and I told him. He's locked up so there isn't much he can do. But I promised him that I would find Talisa and bring her home."

"I can't believe that Talisa is really alive." Precious exhaled. "What's more surprising is you're the one that's helping Genesis. The two of you barely spoke to one another even when Aaliyah and Amir were dating."

"Nico and Lorenzo were close to Genesis and

of course they ain't no friends of mine," Supreme remarked. "But besides that he's always been a decent dude. Plus, Genesis has always looked out for you, so I'm trying to look out for him too. It's only right."

"I think that's sweet." Precious leaned over and kissed Supreme on his shoulder before laying her head on it. "I remember when Genesis told me he thought his wife might be alive. I highly doubted it, but I couldn't bring myself to say that to him because I could look in his eyes and tell how desperately he wanted it to be true. But he was right. Wow, talk about a miracle."

"Yeah, it is. I've had a couple of private investigators working on things for me and one of them found a location. I'm hoping she's still there."

"Me too. My goodness wait until Skylar finds out." Precious's head started throbbing at the very thought.

"She already knows. I told her."

"Why did you do that?" She cringed."You should've let Genesis tell her. She has to be heartbroken."

"I thought she might know something that could help me find Talisa. I still think she does, but at this point it's pointless."

"Why would Skylar know anything?"

"Because the same person that was responsible for taking her, took Talisa."

"Arnez!" Precious scoffed. "That man is evil. Him and Maya was truly a match made in hell. The world is a much safer place without the two of them conspiring together," Precious said rolling her eyes.

"It's hard for me to believe that Arnez kidnapped Talisa and Skylar, but had them in different locations," Supreme reasoned.

"It's possible. We're talking about Arnez. There's nothing logical about the way he think," Precious argued.

"Maybe you're right, but my gut is telling me something different. It doesn't matter though."

It matters to me, Precious thought to herself, but choosing not to share that info with Supreme. "I hear you." Precious sighed. "I can't lie though, these last couple of weeks have been craycray. First Nico got shot, then we find out he has a grown daughter and now Talisa is alive. I can only imagine what's coming next."

"Who you telling. I don't know why Nico having another daughter caught me by surprise," Supreme said tossing a few more items in his bag.

"Maybe because she appeared out the blue.

If it wasn't for the fact that Nico had a DNA test I would think this was some sort of joke."

"I'm sure Aaliyah wishes it was a joke." Supreme chuckled. "I spoke to her a few days ago and she doesn't seem too pleased about having a younger sister."

"I know. It is sorta funny. Aaliyah is used to being the only girl, sharing has never really been her thing."

"I wonder where she gets that from?" Supreme mocked before laughing some more.

"I'll admit, I'm a piece of work and so is our daughter. But eventually Aaliyah will come around to the idea of having a sister. It might take her some time, but it will all work out." At least Precious hoped it would.

Chapter Six

Weak Link

When Lorenzo arrived to the plush estate in a suburb on the outskirts of Philly, he was impressed with how well Delondo was doing for himself.

"I'm here to see Delondo," Lorenzo told the security guard at the front gate.

"Your name?"

"Lorenzo. Delondo is expecting me."

The security guard placed a call getting the

approval to open the gate. Lorenzo drove up the circular driveway, anticipating getting the information he needed from Delondo so he could figure out who was the Fed's star witness. When he got out his car there was another security guard waiting for him. They entered through the double mahogany doors and that was only the beginning of the sophisticated home.

Once inside of the grand foyer you couldn't help but be amazed at the three story, steel and wood, free-floating custom circular stairway. The first floor was highlighted by a professional office with wet bar and door into a temperature controlled mahogany wine cellar. On the second floor there was immense spaciousness, dramatic 12ft ceiling heights, and breathtaking floor to ceiling windows sprawled across three exposures. The living area featured an ebony wood entertainment center and gas fireplace, while the dining area was highlighted with four floor to ceiling windows and brilliant chandelier.

A sunroom that overlooked the garden, created the ambiance of living within a green oasis. The custom kitchen had Australian cabinetry, top of the line stainless steel appliances, English faucets, a custom, unique stainless steel backsplash, and an island bar counter with

French granite countertop. There was even an ultimate game room in the basement with a complete caterer's kitchen.

"To say I'm impressed would be an understatement," Lorenzo commented to Delondo. "You have immaculate taste," he continued, surprised at how elegant and refined the home was.

"Thank you, but I can't take credit. My wife is the one with the design skills," Delondo said and as if right on cue she came walking out.

"Are you talking about me." She smiled giving Delondo a kiss. As she was about to step away, he pulled her back in closer for another kiss. "Lorenzo, this is my wife Astrid."

"It's a pleasure to meet you," she said extending her long slender hand.

"The pleasure is all mine," Lorenzo countered intrigued by the woman who looked more like a well-polished socialite than the wife of a drug kingpin.

"I'll leave you gentlemen alone to discuss business," she said giving Delondo another kiss. "I'm off to go pick up Delilah."

"Have Milton take you."

"Del, I can drive myself."

"But..."

"I'll be fine," Astrid said cutting Delondo off.

"If you're not here when I get back, once again it was a pleasure meeting you, Lorenzo." His wife exited out in the same grace and ease as when she entered the room.

"You've made quite a life for yourself, Delondo. Beautiful home, wife, and a daughter. All those years ago when we crossed each other's paths a few times, I never would've imagined all this for you. You have definitely made the game work in your favor. Not many can say that."

"Thank you, but don't act like you ain't doing big things, Lorenzo. Don't think I don't know about those heavy ties you have in the music industry. That's a good look. I also know you, Genesis, and Nico are moving major product," Delondo added.

"True, but I'm sure you heard about what's going on with Genesis."

"Of course. There's a small clique of us that's stackin' the paper we make, so when one of our own take a hit, we all know about it."

"You're right and that's why we have to look out for each other too."

"I agree, but man I promise I don't know anything about Genesis's case. If I did I would tell you. I've known that man for a long time. Have mad respect for him. I don't know nothing,"

Delondo let it be known.

"I believe that and that's one of the reasons I'm here."

"I'm following you."

"Genesis asked me to look over the paperwork the Feds turned over to his lawyer. You know, to see if I could pick up on some things that a straight-laced attorney would know nothing about."

"That was smart. Did you find anything?"

"Yeah. The Feds are investigating you."

"Are you sure?" Delondo's voice was composed, but Lorenzo could see fear in his eyes. Lorenzo didn't blame him. He was living the American dream on some next level shit. No way would Delondo want to give all that up.

"One hundred percent. I saw it in black and white. It was the initials D.B and they mentioned a deal that went down in Philly. Come on...you already know."

"Fuck!" Delondo pounded his fist down on the table before taking a seat. "I've been so careful. I haven't personally touched no product in years. My circle is so fuckin' tight. I don't understand this shit."

"I do. Clearly whoever this witness the Feds are keeping anonymous has done business with you and Genesis."

"But I have a direct connect with a cartel in Mexico. I don't believe we get drugs from the same connect," Delondo stated.

"You're right, we don't, but it's somebody. You need to look closely at your crew. Somebody in your circle is working with the federal government. They already got Genesis and you're next on the hit list. I know you ain't ready to give all this up," Lorenze said glancing around Delondo's opulent home.

"I"ma find out who the motherfucker is and they good as dead."

"Good because without them the Feds' case will fall completely apart and Genesis will be able to beat the charges. Not only that, their investigation against you will crumble."

"I hate a disloyal nigga. Everyone in my clique eat good. To become an informant for the government...a fuckin' snitch. Yo!" Delondo's jaw was tight and his face was scowled up. He looked like he was about to transform into a tornado and rip through his crib.

"I understand you angry, but you have to keep your cool. They watching you and right now would be the wrong time to make bad moves, especially the kind that are based on emotion.

We all have to be strategic with this shit. Handle it with caution. Even with your crew. You can't let any of them know your eyes are wide open searching for the weak link."

"Man, that shit gon' be so hard. I can't lie, I'm tempted to go murk my entire crew and start from scratch. I can't be around motherfuckers I can't trust."

"I get it, but that's your emotions talking for you right now. I came to put you on alert and to help me figure out who the informant is. If you start retaliating and lashing out on some terminator type shit, you gon' make it worse. Genesis don't need it and you definitely don't need that."

"You right," Delondo agreed getting his feelings in check. "I gotta make chess moves not checkers."

"Exactly. Right now you have the upper hand because the Feds and the informant think you still sleep. They have no idea you all the way woke which gives you the power so use it wisely," Lorenzo advised not wanting Delondo to do anything that might fuck up Genesis's chances of getting out of prison.

"I booked our flights back to LA. We leave tomorrow," Renny casually mentioned to Nichelle as they were eating breakfast in their hotel room.

"Tomorrow! I'm not ready to leave New York. I haven't even had a chance to see Genesis yet."

"You haven't seen Genesis? What's the hold up?"

"I'm not sure exactly what happened, but his visitation privileges were revoked. Amir spoke to Genesis's attorney the other day and they should be reinstated soon. I'm not leaving until I see him," Nichelle made clear.

"I don't wanna leave you, but I don't like Elijah being with the nanny by himself for this long."

"He loves Millie. She's like a surrogate grand-mother to him."

"That's true, but I think at least one of us should get back to LA. Since you want to see your brother then that leaves me," Renny said, picking up the New York Times and flipping to the business section.

"Okay. You go back to LA and I'll stay here until I know Genesis is okay."

"Don't get too comfortable in NYC," Renny looked up and said. "I want you home."

"I want to be home with you and Elijah, but my brother needs me right now and so does my nephew. While I was visiting him the other day, he got the most bizarre phone call," Nichelle mentioned while reaching in the basket for another bagel.

"What was the phone call about?" Renny asked, not sounding really interested, but simply asking to be polite.

"Someone called saying that my brother's dead wife was alive and that he could have her back for a price."

"Talisa?!" Renny put the newspaper down and stared up at his wife giving her his full attention."

"Yes." She nodded. "Do you know I never even had a chance to meet her, and poor Amir, he never even knew his mother."

"That is bizarre. Does Amir think it was some sort of prank or was it legit?"

"It rattled him. He said a few weeks before Genesis got locked up that he had mentioned Arnez called him saying that Talisa was alive. Of course nobody really believed it was true. They figured Arnez was only trying to fuck with Genesis's head, but who knows." Nichelle shrugged. "Your cousin has proven he is capable of anything."

"Arnez's fixation on destroying Genesis runs deep. He's lost everything, including his life due to his determination to ruin that man."

"Tell me about it. I know firsthand since he killed my mother and tried to kill me too. There's no doubt in my mind that I would've met the same fate as my mother if you hadn't showed up and shot him. Unfortunately, you didn't shoot him dead.

Renny didn't respond to Nichelle's last comment he was too preoccupied thinking about the phone call she mentioned Amir received. It not only got him thinking about Arnez, but also the possibility that it was true. Talisa was alive and all these years she had been held captive by his deranged cousin. Renny couldn't decide if he should just leave it alone or find out if it was true that Talisa was alive.

Chapter Seven

M.I.A...Again

"Precious, thank you for coming," Skylar said giving her a hug.

"Well, I did call you inviting myself over." Precious laughed.

"I know, but I needed the company. My mom took Kyle to the beach while he was out of school for fall break and I've been pretty lonely," she said as the ladies took a seat outside on the balcony, taking advantage of the unseasonably warm day.

"You should've called me. We could've went out for lunch or done some shopping. It's not like I have a ton of things going on. Aaliyah's in Miami getting ready for her wedding, Xavier is off to college, and with Maya being dead now, I'm not as busy as I used to be." Precious giggled with a devilish smile.

"You're such a mess, Precious. I always get a good laugh from you. I thought about calling you, but I didn't want to be a bother."

"Skylar, you would never be a bother. I like you...a lot and I can't say that about many people. I consider you to be a friend," Precious told her and she wasn't lying. In a lot of ways Precious thought of Skylar like a little sister. Ever since they almost died together in the car, when that hit man put a gun to their heads, she was somewhat protective of Skylar.

"Thanks for saying that because I need a friend more than ever right now."

"I'm sure. Genesis being locked up has to be hard on you. You weren't even home that long after being kidnapped and now he's gone."

"It's not only that." Skylar went silent and fidgeted with a magazine on the glass table before continuing. "I'm sure Supreme has told you that Talisa is alive and he's looking for her. He wants to bring Genesis's wife back home to him," Skylar said with contempt in her voice.

"He did mention it to me and I was surprised because, of course, Supreme and Genesis are far from friends. But then immediately after he told me, I thought about you and I was concerned. I know how much you love Genesis."

"And look where that love got me. You warned me not to get caught up in Genesis."

"I did, but not because I thought his dead wife was going to miraculously come back, it was because of his job occupation. Falling in love with a man who runs a lucrative drug empire is always risky."

"Is that why you chose Supreme over Nico?" Skylar questioned.

"That's an interesting question you bring up. Honestly, I never thought about it. Maybe if I had met them at my age now when I have a lot better sense, I would take their occupations into consideration. But way back then none of that mattered to me. I basically did whatever the fuck I wanted to do with whoever I wanted to do it with. Don't get me wrong, I had mad love for Nico and I still do. He will always hold a special place in my heart, but Supreme, he is my heart," Precious said with a sparkle in her eye.

"I know what you mean. It's like I have love for Kyle's dad, but my heart will forever belong to Genesis and now that I'm carrying his child..." Skylar's voice faded off.

"OMG, Skylar! You're pregnant?" That tidbit caught Precious completely off guard.

"Yes."

"Does Genesis know?"

"I told him at my last visitation."

"What did he say?"

"Basically that I should have an abortion and if I do decide to keep the baby then just know that our relationship is over. Because if by some miracle he gets out of jail he plans on spending the rest of his life with Talisa. That about sums it up!" Skylar exclaimed sounding defeated.

"I'm so sorry. That had to be so hard to hear."

"Oh, I forgot one last thing. On a positive note, Genesis said he would financially provide for me and the child." Skylar shook her head. "I always dreamed of falling in love with a man that could take really good care of me, but who knew having that, didn't necessarily mean the man would love me back."

"Skylar, that's where you're wrong. Genesis does love you. He's such a private and guarded man. He would've never moved you here and put you and your son up in this beautiful condo if he didn't love you. I know Genesis and he isn't that sort of man."

"Maybe you're right, but it doesn't change the fact that he clearly loves Talisa a lot more. I wish she could've just stayed on that island," Skylar slipped and said without thinking.

"Island...how do you know that Talisa is on an island?" There was a long eerie pause. "Skylar! Look at me. How do you know Talisa is on an island?" Precious pressed for an answer.

"Because Arnez had us stuck on the same island together," Skylar revealed to a stunned Precious.

Supreme took his private plane and then a helicopter to the small island that the naked eye couldn't even find on a map. He brought a small army with him as another helicopter was occupied with nothing but killers. He had no idea what he was walking into. Only thing he knew was this was Talisa's last known location.

"Based on the information from the private investigator, right over that small bridge is where the housing is," Trigger, one of Supreme's security details said as they all headed in that direction. Everyone including Supreme was armed and ready to shoot to kill if necessary. It was a short walk to the bridge. Once the men walked over it they entered what first appeared to be a little piece of paradise. Three cabanas were all a few feet away from a beach with white sand and sparkling clear blue water that demanded you to take a dip. From a distance you could see what looked to be a main house as it was much larger than the cabana. There were exotic trees and flowers that outlined a walking trail that seemed to go around the entire island.

"The two of you come with me to search those cabanas, the rest of you go search that main house," Supreme ordered. When they entered the cabanas they looked more like a place for a romantic retreat than of a prison.

"Boss, I think I found something," one of the security men said. He was holding up a bikini that was lying on the bathroom floor next to the shower. That was the only thing that seemed to be left behind in the cabanas that were each decorated in all white from the sheer curtains and throw rugs to the bed linen.

"Let's go see if they found anything up at the main house," Supreme said as they exited out.

But once they got there they found nothing.

"The kitchen was fully stocked with food, but all the bedrooms and everything else was empty. There was a toothbrush left in one of the bedrooms. But it seems like everything was cleared out and it wasn't that long ago," Trigger said.

Supreme stood in the entrance seething. "Somehow whoever has Talisa must've found out that we were on to them and about to make a move. Fuck! How am I gonna tell Genesis that once again Talisa is missing," Supreme said shaking his head in disgust.

Chapter Eight

Closer To Home

"Glad I'm finally able to see you again. So much has happened since the last time we talked," Amir said sitting across from his father. "Why did they shut down your visitations anyway? Your attorney was acting like he didn't know what happened."

"Man, they in here fuckin' wit me. When Skylar came to see me I grabbed her arm. It was only for a second, but the guard made a big deal about it and they used that as an excuse to put my visitation on hold," Genesis huffed. "If it wasn't for Meissner pulling some strings, I still wouldn't have no visitation privileges. They some real dicks up in here."

"I'll be so damn happy when you outta this place. You don't belong here," Amir scoffed.

"Don't get ahead of yourself. Son, I always try to be honest with you and there's a very good chance I won't be getting out. You have to prepare yourself for that," Genesis stressed. He could tell Amir wasn't trying to hear that so he changed the subject. "So you said a lot has been going on...like what?"

"For one, Nico got shot."

"What! Is he okay?"

"Yeah, he made a full recovery. He had to get surgery and he was in a coma for a few days, but he's out the hospital now."

"Thank goodness. We don't need no more losses."

"I know that's right."

"Who shot him?"

"Not sure. It happened in Miami. I do know whoever the dude was, he's dead. But wait...did you know Nico has another daughter? Justina told me."

Genesis nodded his head yes. "That must mean Nico finally located her. Good for him." He smiled.

"Why didn't you tell me?"

"It wasn't my place. Only a couple people knew. His own daughter didn't even know. Once Nico found out about her, he spent months trying to locate her."

"Wow, that's nice. I'm happy for him. Not sure if Aaliyah is happy about it but..."

"They'll work it out. Aaliyah understands the importance of family. If she doesn't, Nico will remind her." Genesis laughed. "So is that it or is there more going on?"

"Nichelle is in New York."

"I told you not to tell her, Amir."

"Dad, I didn't. She heard about it through the news. She caught a flight the moment she got word. She wants to see you."

"Damn, I don't want my baby sister to see me here...like this."

"I know you think of her as your baby sister, but she's a grown woman, Dad. Nichelle wants to be here for you Dad and you should let her. Personally, I'm glad she came. She's been really supportive especially after I received a phone call a few weeks ago."

"A phone call...from who?"

"I don't know, but they called on your phone. I let the guy think I was you because I wanted to know what he was talking about," Amir said.

"So what did he say?"

"He said you all had a mutual friend named Gabe."

"Gabe?" Genesis questioned, as that name wasn't ringing any bells.

"Yes. He said you had paid this Gabe dude some money and you would have to give him double if you wanted Talisa back. Then he hung up. I haven't heard anything from him since. I guess it was some sort of sick prank."

"No, it wasn't," Genesis said rubbing his forehead. "I remember who the dude Gabe is now. That's the man I paid to get Skylar back. They must have Talisa too."

"Are you telling me that my mother is alive?" Amir's eyes widened with skepticism.

"I didn't want to say anything until Supreme brought her home."

"Supreme! What does Supreme have to do with anything?"

"When I first got locked up he came to see me. During the time he found the information proving Maya was behind everything and working with Arnez, he also found out that Talisa was in fact alive."

"Why didn't you tell me?"

"Because that pain I see in your eyes right now, I wanted to spare you from that. Because if Supreme can't bring her home that pain will turn to devastation."

"I don't need you protecting me. I'm a grown man. I ain'ta little boy. If my mother is alive then it should be me out there looking for her not Supreme!"

"Keep your voice down," Genesis shot back. "I already told you these people got it out for me. You in here being loud ain'tgon' do nothing but give them another reason to fuck wit me and my visitations."

"I'm sorry, Dad."

"Son, I know finding this out is hard for you. Don't you think I wanna be out there looking for your mother? I feel useless being caged up in here. Supreme didn't have to volunteer to go find Talisa, but he did and I'll be eternally grateful. You should be too."

"You're right and I am. I just wish I could be the one to help him."

"If you wanna help him, tell Supreme about that phone call you received. If they have your mother then Supreme might be able to track them down. He has connections and access to people that you can't get to."

"Point taken. I'll go to Supreme and I'll help him anyway I can. I never imagined I would be able to see my mother, or touch her, alive in front of my face. I'll do whatever necessary to bring her home safely."

"Good because I have a feeling it's gonna take all of us working together to make that happen," Genesis stated.

Talisa went from being held captive in the tranquility of a beachfront paradise to a rundown house in the middle of nowhere. She could no longer look out and see luscious waves from the sapphire deep blue sea. Or hear the chirps from the birds, feel the calming breeze, or eat fresh fruits and vegetables. It was those things that made being a prisoner tolerable for Talisa, but now they had all been ripped away.

"Here, eat this," Mario said tossing down some random fast food on the table. Talisa opened the white paper bag and frowned at the greasy burger and fries.

"No, thank you," she said politely pushing the bag away.

"Fine. Starve if you want to." Mario shrugged plopping down on the dingy couch and turning on the television.

"How long are we going to be here?" Talisa was hesitant to ask the question, but she desperately wanted to know. The stench from the shabby surroundings was enough for her to toss her reluctance out the window.

"You don't like the new digs?" Mario gave an ingenious chuckle. "It may not be a private island, but it could be worse."

"Does that mean I'm going to be here for awhile?"

"That depends."

"Depends on what?"

"How much you're worth. For your sake it better be a lot and they better have the money," Mario said turning his attention back to the television.

Mario and Julio had been ready to get rid of Talisa right after they placed their phone call weeks ago. The only hold up was the two men deciding how much they planned to ask for. They forgot to get that information before killing Gabe so they were left with trying to figure it out on their own. Julio made the decision to do a google search on Genesis Taylor hoping that would give them an idea of how much he was worth. It was then the numerous articles came up regarding Genesis's arrest, which caused the men to panic. If Genesis had been in a federal prison then whom did Julio speak with on the phone. It was then they decided it was time to flee the island. Now here they were in what was the equivalent of a shack trying to decide what they're next move should be.

Talisa sat and observed Mario sitting on the couch laughing at whatever he was watching on television. He seemed content and comfortable in their new surroundings. She then wondered what he meant when he said it depended on how much she was worth. It was the first time any mention of money and her freedom had been spoken of. There were only two people that she could think of that had money and would care about her return, that was her dad and her husband. But so many years had passed and in the back of her mind she wondered if they even cared. Their lives had moved on, but hers had stood still.

Talisa had become so immersed in her thoughts that at first she didn't realize that Julio had walked in. It wasn't until he came near the table she was sitting at that Talisa snapped out of her daydreaming. Julio glanced down at the un-eaten food on the table then turned his attention to Mario.

"I need to talk to you," Julio said to Mario who was too busy laughing at whatever he was watching."I saidI need to talk to you!" Julio barked turning off the television.

"Man, why you turn that off?" Mario jumped up so he could turn the TV back on.

"I told you we need to talk."

"Then talk."

"Not here," Julio said glancing over at Talisa who was doing her best to pretend she wasn't paying attention to the interaction going on in front of her. "Let's go in the back."

Mario nodded his head and followed behind Julio. Talisa waited until she heard the door close before sneaking off to find out what was going on. She put her ear near the door so she could hear their conversation clearly.

"But I'm not sure how to handle it," Talisa heard Julio say, catching the end of his sentence. She leaned in closer wanting to make sure she caught the entire dialogue exchange.

"You need to figure out how you want to

handle it soon. We can't keep her here forever."

"I know this, but we have to be careful. What if it was a Fed that answered Genesis's phone? They could be tracking us," Julio said becoming paranoid.

"Nah, I don't think it was a Fed," Mario disagreed.

"Why not? The Feds have him now on all those drug charges. Maybe they took his phone trying to monitor his calls to see who he's doing business with."

"Or maybe it was one of his business associates who he gave his phone to before getting locked up," Mario countered. "Based on the charges he's facing, it seems like the Feds already built a solid case before they arrested him. They don't need that man's phone."

"You have a point, but why did the caller pretend he was Genesis Taylor? Why didn't he say who he really was?"

"There's only one way to find out. Call and ask him. Listen, we need to stop wasting time. You made us pack our shit up and leave the island. We didn't kill Gabe so we could be stuck in this dump. If you ain'tgonna make a move, then we need to go ahead and get rid of the girl and cut our losses. We can't afford to take care of her,"

Mario spat.

"When you say get rid of her do you mean kill her?" Julio questioned.

"What the hell else would I mean? We can't just let her go if we ain't gettin' nothin' in return."

"Arnez was adamant that we couldn't kill her," Julio said.

"Where the fuck is Arnez at now! We ain't heard from that nigga in months. He might be dead for all we know. You kept your word not to kill her when we had money to take care of this woman and we were being compensated. That is no longer the case. So you either sell her off or we must get rid of this dead weight."

"Fine, I will make the phone call. But if I think this is some sort of set up with the Feds then we're getting the hell out of New York," Julio made clear.

"I'm wit' that, but we leaving without the girl."

"Of course," Julio agreed.

Talisa tiptoed away as fast as she could without being heard. Her heart was racing with all the information she heard. First, she couldn't believe she was in New York. They kept her blindfolded and handcuffed until they reached the destination. They were so far out in a desolate location that it could've been anywhere. Knowing she was in New York made Talisa feel like she was getting closer to home.

Then learning that Genesis was locked up broke Talisa's heart. Even if she did manage to get free, prison would now be the obstacle keeping them apart. But in Talisa's mind being able to talk and see her husband again was all that mattered. She would take loving Genesis behind prison walls over never seeing his face again.

Chapter Nine

No More Lies

Delondo stared up at the dome ceiling in the master bedroom. The wood-burning fireplace was meant to relax him, but instead it heightened Delondo's stress.

"Baby, what's wrong?" Astrid asked when she came and sat down next to her husband on the bed. "You haven't been yourself lately. Come to think of it, your mood has been off ever since that man, Lorenzo, came to see you."

"I'm fine. It's business stuff that's all."

"Delondo, you don't have to lie to me. I'm your wife. You can tell me anything," she assured him. Delondo continued looking up at the ceiling before getting off the bed and opening up the double doors that led to the balcony.

Astrid remained on the bed for a few minutes debating whether to give her husband some alone time or pressing the issue. She chose to press on.

"Instead of having me behave like a nagging wife, you should come clean and save me from becoming annoying," Astrid joked.

"A little humor is always good." Delondo chuckled.

"At least I was able to turn that frown into a smile. That means we're making progress."

"We are." Delondo pulled his wife in for an embrace, holding her tightly. "You know you're the best thing that has ever happened to me. I don't know what I would do if I didn't have you in my life."

"That's never going to happen so you don't have to worry about that. You're stuck with me." She smiled kissing her husband's soft lips. Astrid thought back to the first time she saw Delondo. They were both attending a private wine tasting at a restaurant in downtown Philly. After accidentally spilling her drink on his slacks, instead of Delondo being angry he asked her out to dinner. Astrid was drawn to the handsome man with a roughneck demeanor and couldn't resist accepting his invite. That dinner date turned into a proposal, marriage, and a child that they shared together.

"I hope you mean that because I need your loyalty more than ever right now," Delondo said releasing Astrid from his embrace.

"You're scaring me, Delondo. What is going on?"

"There's no easy way to say this." Delondo turned away and placed his hands down on the balcony, pressing down firmly on the stone banister. He stared out at the immaculate garden that sprawled across the property, complete with a koi pond and mature shrubbery/trees with a covered walkway. But all that beauty nature had to offer couldn't ease Delondo's mind. "I'm on the Feds radar," he exhaled and said.

"What!? You have to be mistaken."

"It's no mistake. That's what Lorenzo came over to talk to me about. His partner Genesis is locked up right now. While going over his paperwork he found out they're building a case against me right now."

"How long have they been investigating you?"

"I'm not sure, but the investigation is ongoing and I'm positive someone in my inner circle is cooperating with the Feds. Never did I think one of my guys would be a snitch," Delondo admitted with disappointment.

"Do you have any idea who it might be?" Astrid questioned, placing her hand lovingly on her husband's shoulder.

"Nope. Ever since Lorenzo left here that day, I've been racking my brain trying to figure this shit out."

"What have you come up with?"

"Only that it has to be either Capo, Theron, Lex, or Harvey. They are the only ones high enough on the totem pole that would have useful information to give to the Feds. But I can't figure out which one is that fuckin' weak," Delondo said through clenched teeth, balling up his fist.

"Baby, you have to calm down. Getting upset isn't going to make this case the Feds are building against you go away."

"True, but killing whoever is running they fuckin' mouth will. I have to figure who it is and fast before I lose everything I love the most which is you and our daughter."

"You'll never lose us. We're a family...forever."

"We can't be no family if I'm doing twenty to life behind bars. I won't let that happen even if it means wiping out every member of my crew," Delondo stated without flinching.

Precious was taking a much needed hot bubble bath while sipping on some Riesling and listening to soft classical music. The classical music was only a recent discovery for Precious. In his will Quentin left his prized collection to his daughter. At first she had wondered why he left it to her since that wasn't exactly in her top three genre choices. But Precious then remembered that rare occasion when she was having brunch with her father and he mentioned when he had a lot on his mind and needed to shut himself off from the rest of the world, listening to classical music was his escape. As the warmth of the water relaxed Precious's body, it was the music that soothed her soul and she had to admit that Quentin had been right. That memory made her smile and for a quick second, shifted her thoughts off of the conversation she had with Skylar the other day.

As if reading her mind, Precious realized her cell was ringing and when she picked it up off the chair next to the bathtub she saw it was Skylar.

"Gosh, why didn't I turn my phone off," Precious sighed before answering. "Hello."

"I'm so glad you answered. I haven't stopped thinking about what we discussed since you left." Skylar sighed.

"Then we're both having the same problem because I can't stop thinking about it either."

"You haven't told Supreme have you? Or Genesis? Please tell me you haven't told Genesis!" Skylar exclaimed.

"Take it down a notch. I haven't told Supreme and I haven't spoken to Genesis so no, but..."

"But nothing, Precious!" Skylar yelled cutting her off. "You can't tell Genesis or no one else!"

"Girl, you gon' stop yelling in my ear. I know that much," Precious popped.

"I'm sorry. I shouldn't be yelling at you."

"No, you shouldn't."

"I'm just so frazzled and being pregnant is doing absolutely nothing to help keep my emotions in check," Skylar huffed.

Although it had been many years since Precious had been with child, she had vivid memories of how emotional she had been during both of her pregnancies. For that reason she was understanding of Skylar's temperament.

"Skylar, I won't tell Genesis what we talked about, but you have to know he will find out. Once Supreme brings Talisa home the two of you will eventually see each other and she'll realize you left her on that island, knowing that she was Genesis's wife. So you don't have to worry about me telling him because Talisa will do it for me."

"What if Talisa doesn't come back. Just because Supreme is looking for her doesn't mean he'll find her."

"You didn't kill her before you left did you?" Precious raised up from the water in a panic. "Answer me!"

"Of course not! I'm not a murderer, Precious."

"Thank goodness." Precious leaned back getting comfortable in the bathtub, relieved she didn't have to add killer to Skylar's resume. "Being crazy in love makes people do absurd things. Trust me, I know." Precious rolled her eyes before taking the rest of her wine to the head.

"I am deeply in love with Genesis. I wish we could raise our child together and be a family. There is no doubt in my mind that would happen if Talisa stayed out of the picture."

"But Talisa is in the picture. His wife is alive

and you tried to keep her dead. Genesis will be pissed the fuck off when he finds out you lied to him about something so important."

"There's nothing I can do about that now."

"You can tell him the truth before Talisa does."

"Or you?"

"Skylar, I told you I wouldn't tell Genesis and I'm a woman of my word."

"What about Supreme? If you tell him you know he's going to tell Genesis."

"Honestly, Supreme is already suspicious of you. I thought he was reaching when he told me he felt you were hiding something, but he was right. I won't tell Supreme, but Skylar, secrets like this always come out. You should tell Genesis the truth before it gets ugly."

"I hear you, Precious, but things have already gotten ugly. I'm going to lose the man I love to either jail or another woman. It can't get any uglier than that," Skylar reasoned.

"That's where you're wrong," Precious shot back, closing her eyes wishing she wasn't privy to any of Skylar's bullshit.

Chapter Ten

Mistakes Can't Be Made

"Supreme, thanks for seeing me on such short notice. I know you have a lot going on," Amir said when he arrived at Supreme's office in Midtown.

"You said it was important. What can I do for you?" Supreme asked dryly, sitting down on a couch that had a wide sweep view of historical landmarks in New York City.

"It is. I went to see my father and he told me that my mother was alive."

"I'm surprised he told you. He said he wanted to keep things contained until we were able to bring her home."

"He only told me because I received a phone call about my mother. The man called my father's phone and when I answered he assumed I was him."

"What did the caller say?" Supreme leaned forward, listening intently.

"He said that my father had done business with a dude named Gabe and he wanted double for the return of my mother. I thought it was some sort of sick joke. That's the only reason my father told me what was going on."

"Amir, you need to keep what's going on to yourself. As few people as possible needs to know about your mother being alive right now."

"I understand. I can keep things to myself," Amir said warily.

"Are you sure about that?"

"What is that supposed to mean?" Amir questioned defensively.

"Meaning that you seem to have a problem keeping important information to yourself."

Amir bit down on his lip and put his head

down. "This is about me telling Aaliyah about Emory. I made a mistake. It was an accident."

"That was no mistake or accident. You let your jealousy over Aaliyah's relationship with Dale get the best of you. You were hoping by telling her it was me that killed Emory, it would ruin whatever they had."

"Maybe you're right," Amir hated to admit.

"I know I'm right. You're still young and I understand you might find it difficult to keep your emotions in check, but we can't afford to make mistakes that might put your mother's life in further jeopardy," Supreme stated.

"I would never do that!" Amir retorted, becoming upset. "I want my mother home and like I told my father, I'll do anything to help you to make that happen."

"Good. You can start by giving me some information because I haven't spoken to your father since I got back."

"Wherever you went did it have something to do with my mother?"

"Yes. My people had got a location on her. But when we got there the island was deserted. We could tell they vacated the property recently. As if they got word we were coming and had to leave quickly. That's why it's so important we keep things quiet."

"I agree. Damn! I can't believe you were so close to finding my mom."

"It was frustrating to me too. I don't want to tell your father. He has enough to deal with. But I would like to know who this Gabe person is."

"My dad told me that he paid Gabe for Skylar's return."

"Interesting. You haven't heard anything else from the man?"

"No and it's been a few weeks now. I'm surprised because he wanted money for her return, but I've heard nothing." Amir shrugged.

"You said the caller thought you were your father...right?"

"Yeah, but why does that matter?"

"Maybe he found out that your father is locked up so there was no way he was talking to Genesis Taylor," Supreme rationalized.

"I didn't even think about that, but it would make sense."

"It would also explain why they packed up and got the hell outta there so fast." Supreme nodded, feeling like that was exactly what happened. "There's still a very good chance that the man will call back. They want the money."

"What if he doesn't call back?" Amir was

unable to disguise the fear in his voice.

"We found her once, we'll find her again," Supreme spoke with confidence. But on the inside he was praying it wasn't too late.

Julio was outside sitting in his car smoking a cigarette when he finally built up enough nerves to dial Genesis's phone number again. He couldn't shake the feeling that maybe the Feds were the ones that had his phone and this would end up backfiring on him. Then the other part of Julio wanted to believe that maybe Mario was correct and he was letting his paranoia get the best of him.

Besides the potential payday that was waiting for them if it turned out that whomever he had spoken to would indeed pay the ransom, there was something else that was motivating Julio to make the call. With each passing day Mario was becoming more anxious. The current poor conditions they were living under had his already short temper exploding over the simplest things. Julio was growing concerned that at any moment he would snap and harm Talisa. What Mario didn't understand was that although there was an excellent chance that Arnez was dead, his connections were far-reaching. He was given strict orders to never kill Talisa and Julio wanted to do everything in his power to follow those orders. He didn't want to take any chances that he would suffer some sort of repercussion for not doing what Arnez said.

After taking one last puff, Julio tossed the cigarette out the window and made his call. After the fourth ring, he was about to hang up, but then stopped when he heard a voice on the other end of the phone.

"Hello!" Amir sounded out of breath when he answered. He was in the kitchen when he first heard the phone ringing and had to rush to answer not wanting to miss any calls.

"Who is this?" Julio asked. There was a slight pause as he heard the caller about to speak, but Julio wanted to put a halt to any bullshit. "Before you answer that question, I know Mr. Taylor is in a federal prison. So who am I speaking to? If you're a federal agent, I ain't got nothing to do with no illegal dealings. I'm simply checking up on an old friend of mine," Julio lied, trying to cover his ass.

"I am Mr. Taylor...Amir Taylor. Genesis is my father."

A smiled crept across Julio's face as he realized that payday was still within his reach. "It's a pleasure to speak with you, Amir."

"Save the bullshit. Do you still have my mother? That's all I want to know."

"I'm impressed with your directness. To answer your question, yes, I do have your mother. Do you have my money?" Julio countered.

"I do, just name your price."

"Don't make this difficult," Julio stated before letting Amir know how much he wanted.

After telling Amir the price, Julio expected him to try and negotiate the price, but instead he said, "Okay. Let me know how to get you the money and when you'll bring my mother to me. Understand one thing. If you fuck me over and anything happens to my mother, you're a dead man," Amir said matter-of-factly.

"You talkin' a lot of shit for a man that has no power."

"That's where you're wrong. See, I've never met my mother a day in my life. You're selling me a dream right now and I'm willing to buy it. But if for some reason you're lying to me and you don't bring me my mother, then I'll have to deal with my dream being deferred. You, on the other hand, knows how great it feels to be alive so

I doubt you're looking forward to feeling death. I'm also sure you want to experience being able to buy whatever you want before you die. I'm the person who now gets to decide both of those things. So that gives me the power. Now bring my mother to me." Julio hadn't expected such boldness from the young man. He wasn't sure if he should be scared or excited that soon he would be a rich man.

"The exchange will be made tomorrow. I'll be calling you back shortly with the time and place we'll meet." With that Julio hung up the phone and immediately ran into the house to tell Mario the good news.

When he got inside Julio could hear screaming coming from the back. He ran to the bedroom and saw Mario standing over Talisa with his pants down.

"What are you doing!" Julio barked, knocking Mario down. "Get away from her."

Talisa quickly moved off the bed, using the bed sheet to cover the clothes that Mario had almost completely ripped off her.

"Why you protecting her!" Mario scoffed. "Arnez hasn't given us any money in months. We take care of her. She need to start paying her debt," Mario spit pulling up his pants.

"You cannot rape her! I spoke to her son and he agreed to give us the money! We will get nothing if anything bad happens to her," Julio yelled, pointing his finger at Mario.

"You spoke to my son?" Talisa asked trying to contain her tears.

"Yes, I did," Julio said looking over at her. The fear he saw in Talisa's eyes made Julio feel like shit. He was a lot of things, but a rapist wasn't one of them. "I'm so sorry this happened to you. I promise Mario will never come near you again."

"Thank you," Talisa said, relieved that Julio had shown up when he did. In a few more minutes Talisa had no doubt in her mind that Mario would've been thrusting himself inside of her.

"Let's go, Mario!" Julio ordered, fuming at what he had done. "You are about to ruin everything!" Julio said angrily as they headed into the front room.

"How was I supposed to know you were gonna grow some balls and finally demand the money we deserve," Mario shouted, slumping down on the couch. "You can calm down though, nothing happened wit' that girl."

"She's a grown woman and if I hadn't come into that bedroom when I did you would've raped her. Not only is that sick, but you would've written both of our death certificates. I'm not gonna let you ruin this because you can't control yo' dick!"

"I almost fucked up, but we straight now," Mario said wanting to move on from what just went down. Julio slit his eyes at Mario, tempted to cut him out the deal by simply killing him right then. The only reason he didn't go through with it was because Mario was his first cousin and his mother was Julio's favorite aunt.

"Fine, but Mario,don't ever cross that line again. Are we clear?"

"Yeah, we clear man. Now tell me what dude said? I wanna know how much money we about to be spending." Mario grinned ready to start living the good life.

Chapter Eleven

Almost Home

"All my men are in place. If anything seems off, you press this button on the watch," Supreme explained showing Amir. "My men will attack. Do you understand?"

"Yes. We've been over this three times. I know what to do, Supreme. I won't mess this up," Amir promised.

"You can't mess up," Supreme stressed. "This might be our last opportunity to get Talisa back."

"I can't believe in just a couple hours I'll hold my mother for the very first time." Amir smiled.

"I'm happy for you, Amir. Family is the most important thing. Having the love of your mother is going to change your life. But best believe throughout all these years, a day didn't go by that your mother didn't think of you and keep you close to her heart."

"I appreciate you saying that, Supreme. Not sure why, but you've really stepped up for my father and me. I know he's already thanked you, but I want to say thank you too."

"Let's not get ahead of ourselves, Amir," Supreme patted his shoulder. "Don't thank me until we bring your mother home safely."

"Everything's in order. We have the money, you got your men in place, why do you seem uneasy?"

"Because I knew Arnez personally. I know how his mind works. He's a sick motherfucker, but also very smart and very calculating. I'm assuming the man that has been in contact with you used to work for Arnez before he died. Which means he's sick and calculating too. To what degree we don't know, that's where my uneasiness comes from." Supreme sighed.

"Now is my turn to tell you not to worry. I do

understand your concern, butI can feel it in my heart," Amir said patting his chest. "My mother is coming home and all will go smoothly."

"Then we better get outta here. I wanna make sure my men are in place and that the covert audio is working correctly. Let's go." Supreme grabbed his jacket as he and Amir headed out the door to bring Talisa home.

Talisa woke up with the worse headache. It was so bad that for the first few minutes she couldn't remember what happened to her the night before. But the memories all came flooding back like a freight train that wouldn't stop.

"I want you to get a good night sleep because tomorrow you're going home to your family," Julio told Talisa as she sat on the bed.

Talisa sat speechless. She didn't believe what Julio was telling her could be true. She wouldn't let herself believe it because for so long she had suppressed allowing herself to feel that level of joy. To open her heart to that would mean her nightmare was over.

"Talisa, did you hear what I said? Tomorrow you're going home," Julio said again in case it didn't register the first time.

"Please don't be cruel. I think we can both agree that I've been through enough," Talisa finally spoke up and said.

"I'm not being cruel. I've made contact with your son today and we're taking you to him tomorrow."

"I don't know if I should cry or smile."

"I prefer you smile." Julio grinned. "You get a good night's sleep because tomorrow your new life will begin."

"Yes, it does." Talisa beamed.

"You keep the door locked. I don't want anything happening to you," Julio said leaving out. He meant that too, but it wasn't tjust for his own selfish financial reasons, although that was his biggest motivation. He also agreed with what Talisa said. She had been through enough. Julio was the third watchdog that had been hired to look after Arnez's prized prisoner. Around the seven-year mark he let each man go because they would all soften up to Talisa and begin to feel guilty for keeping her on that island. Julio lasted the longest, but recently he was feeling the same way. With the fucked up predicament she was forced into, Talisa remained sweet, polite, and kind to everyone hired to watch over her including Julio.

When Julio left, Talisa jumped up and locked her bedroom door. She knew he was speaking of Mario when he said he didn't want anything happening to her and neither did she. Talisa wanted to do a happy dance after hearing she was going home tomorrow. Her life was truly about to begin again. Talisa got back in the bed and soon after fell asleep with a smile on her face.

A few hours later that smile vanished when Talisa was awoken by loud noises. She glanced over at the clock and saw that it was 2:15 in the morning. She tried to close her eyes and go back to sleep, but the commotion got even louder. Talisa got out of bed, unlocked, and opened the door with caution. That's when she saw five armed men wearing black ski masks yelling at Julio and Mario. A few minutes later two of the ski-masked men fired off shots killing Julio and Mario instantly. Talisa's heart dropped. She rushed back into the bedroom and locked the door. She looked around to see where she could hide and decided to slide under the bed.

Talisa could hear them trying to open the door. When they realized it was locked they started trying to kick it down. Talisa buried her face in her hands to prevent them from hearing any sounds that she might make. It was like she was playing a part in the movie *Don't Breathe*. But all the not breathing in the world couldn't save Talisa. Before long the door was kicked down and she was being dragged from under the bed. They held her down and the last thing Talisaremembered was feeling a sharp needle being put in her arm.

Now here it was the next day. But Talisa didn't wake up in that raggedy, run down shack she had been stashed in. Instead, she woke up in a plush king-sized bed with percale weave sheets that had decorative hemstitching details. The bedroom was bright from the sunlight coming through the huge floor to ceiling windows. In less than twenty-four hours she went from living in the slums to being in opulence. If it wasn't for Talisa remembering the ordeal she witnessed and going through it herself, she might've thought she was finally home.

"Good morning," a tall slender built man said when he came into the bedroom. Talisa's eyes widened, pressing her back against the headboard. She recognized the man's face as someone that would visit the island on occasion, but she never knew his name. It was like he would come and check in on things then leave. "No need to be afraid, Talisa. I'm not here to hurt you," he said, seeing the fear in her eyes.

"Then why did they drug me and bring me here?" Talisa asked.

"It was for your own protection. We didn't want you putting up a fight and possibly causing yourself harm as you were being relocated."

"Where am I?"

"Somewhere safe. Not in that dump Julio and Mario had you in."

"But I was supposed to go home today. Go be with my son. Are you going to let me go?"

"I can't do that. But I'll make sure you have everything you need to be comfortable. So relax."

"I don't want to relax! I want to go home!" Talisa screamed as the man began to leave.

"So you know, there is a camera in here so please don't do anything stupid. If you behave you'll be free to watch television, listen to music,do anything you like within the confines of this bedroom. If you choose to give us a hard time then you'll leave me no choice, but to keep you tied up and drugged up. The choice is yours," he said and walked out.

Talisa knew she was being watched and didn't want them to see her break down. So she pulled the bedspread over her head and cried her heart out.

Chapter Twelve

Master Plan

Amir stood on the top level of a parking garage. He had been there waiting for the last two hours refusing to leave although Supreme had told him his mother wasn't coming. Amir refused to accept it. The time continued to pass and as the sun began to set, Amir could no longer escape reality.

"You didn't have to come up here," Amir said when he saw Supreme standing in front of him.

"You could've called like you did the other times."

"Yeah, I could've, but I think you needed more than a phone call. Amir, we'll find your mother and you will get through this."

"Nah, you said this was our last chance."

"I said it might be our last chance and I was wrong. I'm more determined than ever to find her."

"How did you know?" Amir questioned.

"Know what?"

"That she wasn't coming. I mean, when we were in your office I could tell that you didn't think it was gonna happen. How did you know?"

"I wasn't positive. I was hoping I was wrong, but my gut was telling me something different. I can't explain why. But like I told you, these sort of things can always go either way," Supreme explained.

"Damn! Why couldn't it go our way? The man sounded so legit. I really believed he wanted the money," Amir said, confused by the turn of events.

"I'm not sure what happened, but to leave that sort of money on the table, it could only be for a few reasons. The man either never had Talisa, he was expecting to get her, but somehow it fell through or somebody else got to him and shut it down. Whatever the reason is, we're not giving up, Amir. We will find your mother."

"I'm just glad I didn't say anything about this to my father when I spoke to him this morning. If I would've got his hopes up and then had to break the news that the shit didn't work..." Amir shook his head unable to finish his thought. His disillusionment with how it all unfolded made him afraid to remain optimistic.

"Don't let this setback discourage you from moving forward," Supreme said as if reading Amir's mind. "I made that mistake with Precious when Maya made me believe she had left me for Nico. When in all actuality she was being held hostage by Pretty Boy Mike. In situations like this, the enemy is always hoping you'll give up. We can't make an error like that when it comes to your mother."

Amir heard the words coming out of Supreme's mouth, but that didn't change the aching in his heart. In his head, Amir had written down a list of firsts that he would do with his mother. The first on his list was to tell his mother he loved her, but that would now have to wait.

Lorenzo and T-Roc were sitting at a back table in a diner on West 78th Street coming up with what they urgently needed which was a master plan. The two handsome men, sporting five thousand dollar designer suits seemed out of place in the quaint diner. They seemed more appropriately dressed for a Fortune 500 boardroom.

"When I spoke to Delondo the other day he still had nothing. He even made a comment about taking out his entire crew so he could just eliminate the problem," Lorenzo informed T-Roc.

"That's the last thing he needs to do. With him being on the Feds radar it's bad enough he needs to murk the snitch, if he kills his whole crew there won't be no explaining that shit away. The Feds will indict his ass knowing no jury will ever believe that shit was a coincidence. We need to get rid of the snitch so Genesis can get out that hellhole he's in. Whatever Delondo wants to do with his fuckin' team after that is on him," T-Roc scoffed.

"We're in agreement on that. But that's not why I wanted to meet with you today," Lorenzo said fidgeting with his napkin. "I need you to help me with something."

"If it has anything to do with helping Genesis, I'm all in. Whatever it is I'll do it," T-Roc said without hesitation.

"I have the names of Delondo's top men. I've already had a thorough check done on them. One of the men, Theron, might've been doing business with a guy named Markell."

"The Markell I know or knew before he got killed a few months ago?"

"Yes, that Markell." Lorenzo nodded.

"Markell was doing business with Arnez. There is no way Delondo would've cosigned on Theron dealing with anybody that had a connection to Arnez. I'm sure Genesis told you that Arnez shot and almost killed Delondo a few years ago," T-Roc said.

"He did that's why I believe if it's confirmed Theron was meeting up with Markell then more than likely he's the snitch."

"Have you told Delondo?"

"Not yet. Honestly, I don't want him to know until we find out for sure and it's already been handled. If Theron is the weak link, it's better that Delondo doesn't have his blood on his hand, given the Feds are trying to build a case against him."

"True dat. Well I know a few of the dudes Markell would've been in contact with if he was in fact doing business in Philly. I can go down there and ask some questions. If there are answers to be gotten, then I'll get them," T-Roc stated with certainty.

"That's what I wanted to hear. Do you need me to come with you because I can," Lorenzo offered.

"Nah, you stay in New York and handle things here. All of us need to be doing our part. I'll bring a couple of my security with me, but Philly my city...I'll be straight."

Lorenzo and T-Roc left the quaint diner feeling like they had accomplished what they came for. A master plan was in affect.

"I spoke to my brother, but he still won't let me come see him. He claims he doesn't want me to see him locked up. Your father is so freakin' stubborn," Nichelle complained to Amir.

"I know. I'm sorry about that. You came all this way for nothing. I tried to tell my father he needed to see you, but like you said, he's stubborn." Amir shrugged.

"It is frustrating, but I don't feel like I came here for nothing. I got to spend time with my favorite nephew."

"Nichelle, I'm your only nephew." Amir laughed.

"True, but you're still my favorite although soon you'll have a little competition."

"Huh!" Amir raised his eyebrow. "What are you talkin' about...competition?"

Nichelle covered her mouth as if embarrassed. "Maybe I do have a big mouth, but for some reason I thought your father already told you. I wonder if I'm the only one he confided in."

"Confided in you about what? What are you talkin' about, Nichelle?" Amir wanted to know.

"Genesis told me his girlfriend or ex-girlfriend, not sure if they're still together..."

"You mean Skylar?" Amir asked.

"Yes, that's her."

"What about Skylar? Wait...my father told you she was pregnant? Is that what you meant about having competition?" Amir kept shaking his head as what Nichelle had said kicked in. "My dad is having another child...wow. Right when we're finally on the verge of bringing my mom home."

"Amir, I didn't mean to upset you."

"My mom has been through so much. When she comes home she already has to deal with the fact that my dad is in jail, now you're adding a baby to the mix."

"I know these circumstances aren't ideal, but a baby is a blessing, Amir. You're going to be a big brother. There's enough love to go around for your mother and a baby," Nichelle said.

"If you say so." Amir sounded unconvinced.

"I thought it was going to be so difficult for me to accept Elijah knowing that he was conceived because my best friend and the man I loved had sex. But I love that little boy like I gave birth to him myself. He has been the most amazing blessing in my life. Sometimes it's the very things we're most afraid of that turn out to be the best thing that's ever happened to us."

Nichelle, you have such a beautiful heart. I always imagined that my mother has the same sweet soul as you."

"Amir, I think those are the kindest words anyone has ever said to me. I never met your mother, but I've heard nothing but wonderful things. For you to compare me to her in anyway makes me feel extremely special."

"Well you are and because of what you said, I'm gonna try my hardest to be the best big brother ever."

"I'm happy to hear that my words of en-couragement inspired you to do that." Nichelle blushed. "That will mean a lot to your father. Of course we're all praying that he'll beat this case, but for some reason if he's not, that baby will need all of our love even more, but especially yours."

"You're right and I'll be there for my little brother or sister."

"Good. Genesis asked me if I would keep an eye on Skylar. Make sure she's okay and doesn't feel alone during her pregnancy. I'm going to give her a call and hopefully she'll let me stop by to see her sometime this week," Nichelle said.

"That'll be nice. I actually like Skylar. I thought she was good for my father. She seemed to make him happy. If my mother weren't alive and coming home, I would want them to be a family. But my dad never stopped loving my mother and after all these years of being kept apart, they deserve to be together."

"I agree. Your mother is the love of Genesis's life. They shouldn't be denied their second chance at happiness," Nichelle stated. But in the back of her mind she couldn't help but wonder how much of an impact his relationship with Skylar had on him. Because of what they had both endured growing up, Nichelle knew how guarded her brother was and so was she, but not to the extent of Genesis. For him to let Skylar in his life and open his heart to her, Nichelle knew he had to love her deeply even if Genesis didn't want to admit it.

Chapter Thirteen

What I Can Do For You

"How's Nico doing?" Precious asked Aaliyah as she was driving on her way to Guerlain Spa at the Waldorf Astoria.

"He's doing so much better. He's back to his normal self. I actually had dinner with him and Angel the other night."

"Really! I wasn't expecting to hear that, how

exciting. Did you enjoy dinner with your father and sister?"

"It was okay. I mean, she's cool, I guess," Aaliyah said reluctantly.

"Be nice, Aaliyah. I know this is a major change for you, but it means a lot to Nico that his daughters get along. You love your father so much. Think about him."

"Mom, I know you're right, but...forget it, let's talk about something else," Aaliyah said abruptly.

Precious chose not to push her daughter about the issue any further. Aaliyah was stubborn and strong-willed just like her mother so Precious decided to change the subject to something that would put a smile on her face. "How's the wedding planning coming?"

"Great! We found the perfect location. I can't wait for you to come and visit so I can show you. You're going to love it," Aaliyah said with enthusiasm.

"I know that I will. I'll be there in a few weeks unless you changed your mind and want Supreme and me to come to your pre-wedding party. I guess that's what you're calling it," Precious said.

"No, you don't have to come. You put to-gether that beautiful engagement party for us. It was intimate with our family and friends. This is something that one of Dale's friends slash business associates is throwing for us at one of his strip clubs. It's an upscale strip club and I'm sure it will be very nice, but I'll probably only know a handful of people there. It's more of a fun party vibe. I even told Nico not to come, but of course he insisted I invite Angel."

"That makes sense. I hope you did?"

"Yes, and she was very happy. She's coming with her husband."

"That's right. She's married to that boxer guy...right?"

"Yep and not just any boxer, but the champion, Darien Blaze."

"Aaliyah, you sound way too excited," Precious mocked. "Listen, I've been parked in front of this hotel for awhile and valet has been very patient so I'm about to head inside. Call me if you need me and please make an effort to be a great big sister. I love you, baby. Talk to you soon."

"Love you too, Mom."

Precious was trying not to worry about her only daughter, but it was hard. Aaliyah had a good heart, but there was no denying her daughter had been spoiled her entire life. From Supreme to Nico and even Quentin who had all treated her like a pampered princess. Precious's hands weren't clean either. Although she tried to balance the scale by not always letting Aaliyah have her way, she adored her daughter and most of the time gave in to her demands. Precious could only hope that with age, maturity had kicked in and Aaliyah would do the right thing.

When T-Roc arrived in Philly, he wasted no time to meet an associate in the Market East area. When he arrived at the bar on Sansom Street, Jimar was already on his second drink.

"I see you couldn't wait for me," T-Roc remarked, taking off his coat and putting his phone on the table before sitting down.

"You know after making money, drinking is my next passion. Why you think I had you meet me at a bar." Jimar chuckled.

"With age sometimes habits change. I guess that don't apply to you."

"Nah, a few years ago I would already be on the sixth or seventh drink, now I'm just about to have my third. So yeah, some habits have changed...I've slowed down a bit." Jimar grinned. "I see you ain't changed. You still walkin' 'round here wit' yo' Hollywood swag. I ain't no hater. Lookin' good man. I can't lie," Jimar said taking another shot to the head.

"Man, I can't lie neither. You look like shit. I'ma have to blame the alcohol," T-Roc cracked. "We go way back. I don't ever remember you looking so..." T-Roc paused sizing up Jimar's dusty jeans, ill-fitting sweater and old Air Jordans.

"You ain't got to say it. I fell on some hard times. Some young knucklehead kids came in and started taking over. Couldn't get no product and them fools didn't show no respect for an OG," Jimar complained.

"Man, you didn't have nobody that could put you on?" T-Roc questioned, surprised by what he was hearing.

"Markell. That's why it was crazy when you called asking about him. You know I used to run wit' his uncle before he got killed. He was up here in Philly and I ran into him. We sat down, talked. You know he was doing real good for himself. Had a plug that getting him plenty of product. He was gon' put me on...have me back in the game." Jimar beamed as if reminiscing about good times.

"So what happened?"

"What the fuck you think happened? You know that nigga got killed!"

"Oh, so this was recent."

"Yeah." Jimar nodded. "When he saw me he was like I remember you and my Uncle Boogie used to look cold. Always dressed to impress. He said I can't have you out here looking like this. Markell put some money in my pockets right then and said he would be in touch."

"Did he ever get in touch with you?"

"Damn sure did. That nigga kept his word. He was young, but he was a man of his word. He came to Philly a few more times and we met up. He said he was about to partner up with a major player in Philly and he wanted to bring me in. Have me be one of his soldiers. All that shit went to shambles when he got killed. Damn shame." Jimar shook his head. "He was a good dude.

"Did he ever tell you who this major player in Philly he was partnering up with?" T-Roc questioned.

"Sure did. This nigga named Theron. He one of Delondo's main men. I don't know if he was doing some side business or if Delondo was part of the deal too."

"Did Markell ever mention Delondo being a partner?"

"Nope, just Theron and his girl."

"Whose girl?"

"Markell's girl."

"Markell had a girl that was part of his drug business?"

"Yeah," Jimar gave a firm head nod. "Every time he came to Philly she was right by his side except for his last visit. I was surprised. I asked him where she was since they seemed to be glued to the hip. But she was a fine young piece of meat. I wouldn't have let her out my sight neither."

"Do you remember her name?"

"Nah, just that face." Jimar smiled. "Last time I saw him and she wasn't wit' him, he said he planned on asking her to be his wife. Young love. That poor girl was probably devastated when he got killed...so sad," he sighed before continuing. "Since she was one of his partners and seemed to know how to run his business, I was hoping she would call and say she would still put me on."

"I guess that call never came," T-Roc said, intrigued by this new information. It made him wonder if this mysterious girlfriend would know more about Theron and if he was the snitch although T-Roc had pretty much made up his mind that he was.

"No, she never called. So here I am doing petty crimes so I can at least get my drinks," Jimar said cradling another glass.

"I'ma take care of you, Jimar. I'll also plug you in with somebody that..." Just then T-Roc's phone started ringing. He lost his train of thought when he looked down on the table to see who was calling.

"Oh shit! That's her!" Jimar said sounding extra excited pointing at T-Roc's phone.

T-Roc glanced up at Jimar and frowned giving him a what in the fuck are you talkin' about stare. "Hold on a sec." T-Roc got up from the table and walked outside. "Hey, baby girl, how you doing?"

"I'm doing pretty good."

"How's Miami?"

"I'm actually loving it. That's why I was calling you. Aaliyah wants me to stay here with her a little longer while she plans the wedding and stuff so I won't be home next week," Justina told her dad.

"Have you told your mother yet? She's gonna be disappointed, but so am I. The house isn't the same without you. I'm used to your brother being gone, but you're my little girl."

"Daddy, I'm not a little girl anymore."

"You'll always be my little girl and don't you forget it."

"I won't." Justina giggled. "Dad, can you tell Mom? I really don't feel like hearing her beg me to come home. Pleeeeeeease," Justina pleaded.

"Alright, but make sure you call and check in with her. You know how your mother worries and we don't want her having any setbacks. She's made a lot of progress and we wanna keep it that way."

"You're right. I promise I'll check in with her frequently."

"That's my girl. Do you need for me to deposit some money in your account? I'm sure you've already run through the money I gave you before you left."

"No, I'm good, but thanks."

"Okay, but let me know if you change your mind," T-Roc said, shocked that his daughter turned down his money. Justina had the same shopping habits as her mother so that was odd to him.

"I will, Daddy! Love you."

"Love you, too." And just like that Justina was gone. T-Roc went back in the bar and Jimar was doing the same thing he was doing before he left him...drinking.

"I was starting to think you wasn't coming back," Jimar joked now sounding like he had a slight buzz.

"I wouldn't leave you like that. Plus didn't

I say I was gonna take care of you," T-Roc said sitting back down.

"Yeah...yeah...yeah. But back to yo' phone call. How you know Markell's girl?"

"What are you talking about?" T-Roc looked confused.

"When yo' phone rang and that pretty girl's face popped up. I told you I didn't remember that name, but I remembered that face." Jimar winked.

"Are you saying that when my phone rang, the young lady's picture that came up was Markell's girlfriend?"

"That's exactly what I'm saying! You know I'm always gon' be in the no judge zone, but don't you think she's a little bit too young for you? I'm just sayin'." Jimar shrugged, taking another shot of liquor.

"Man, you must be mistaken. That young lady you saw on my phone is my daughter. Ain't no motherfuckin' way she was dating Markell," T-Roc spit. "I suggest you get yo' eyes checked and don't ever speak about my daughter again or we gon' have a serious problem," he warned.

"My fault, boss. You right," Jimar stated sobering up real quick when he saw that fire in T-Roc's eyes. T-Roc's temper was legendary and he was not trying to get on that man's wrong side. "You know I been drinking so I can't even see that well. Now that I'm thinkin' about it, that definitely wasn't the girl I saw Markell with," Jimar lied knowing damn well Justina was the one. But it made Jimar no difference. If he needed to lie to T-Roc so he would throw him a bone, then that's what he would do.

"Now that we got that resolved, let's talk about what I can do for you…" T-Roc leaned back and said as Jimar listened intently.

Chapter Fourteen

So Close Yet So Far

"Hey, baby. I woke up thinking about you and then you call." Nichelle smiled into the phone as if Renny could see her face.

"You sound so sexy. I love your 'just woke up' voice. Make me wanna get on a plane so I can lay in the bed next to you."

"Why don't you come? I'm missing you like crazy."

"I miss you, too."

"Does that mean you're on the way?"

"I wish, but I just got to Philly. I had to handle some business here. Once I'm done, I'll be coming to you."

"When will that be?"

"In a few days. I can't go a day longer than that. I need to feel the inside of my wife." Renny's straight no-chaser response had Nichelle yearning for her husband even more. After all these years of being married, Renny was still the only man that Nichelle wanted to spend the rest of her life with. Her mind, body, and soul belonged to him in every way that mattered. The only thing left to share with him was for them to share a child of their own.

"I need to feel you, too. Hopefully you'll finish up your business in Philly quickly and come be with your wife."

"That's the plan."

"Oh, you know what," Nichelle said remembering something.

"What?"

"When I spoke to Genesis yesterday, he mentioned that T-Roc was in Philly following up on some potential leads that could help his case. You should call him. You and T-Roc were always cool. Maybe you can see him while you're there."

"That's my dude. I'm definitely gonna give him a call. See what T-Roc is up to."

"Make sure you tell him I said hello and make sure you call me tonight. I can't fall asleep if I don't hear your voice."

"You know I'ma call my baby before you fall asleep...don't I always," Renny said.

"Yes." Nichelle giggled wondering if Renny could feel her blushing. "I'll let you go so you can handle your business. Talk to you tonight. Love you."

"Love you too, babe." After Renny hung up,Nichelle got out of bed and headed to the bathroom to take a shower. She was having lunch over at Skylar's place and overslept. Nichelle was looking forward to meeting the woman that was carrying her brother's child.

When they initially spoke on the phone Skylar seemed reluctant about meeting Nichelle, but she soon warmed up to the idea and invited her over. Nichelle didn't want to mess up an already fragile situation by being crazy late so she rushed to get ready. She slipped on some distressed skinny jeans, a cream sweater and chocolate brown thigh high boots. Nichelle pulled her hair in a topknot, dabbed on some lip gloss and sunglasses then headed out her hotel suite.

When Supreme and Amir arrived at the rundown house in the middle of nowhere, Trigger and a few of Supreme's other henchmen were still there, thoroughly going over every inch of the place.

"Damn, it reeks in here!" Supreme commented as he and Amir held their fingers under their noses when they walked through the door.

"I guess we know why it smells so bad in here," Amir said looking at the two dead bodies riddled with bullets, slouched over on the couch.

"You sure this was the last place Talisa was being held?" Supreme questioned Trigger.

"Positive. Wherever she is now, they took Talisa from here."

"Who are the two men?"

"Julio and Mario. Both worked for Arnez and were living on the island with Talisa."

"I guess their services were no longer needed," Amir mocked with dismay.

"Or maybe they crossed the line and paid the price with their lives," Supreme suggested.

"What do you mean?" Amir questioned.

"My guess is they took Talisa and vacated the

island bringing her here until they could ransom her off to you. They've clearly been dead for a while now. How much you wanna bet they were murdered the night before the exchange was supposed to be made. They probably assumed with Arnez being dead they were in the clear to sell Talisa off, but obviously they were wrong," Supreme reasoned.

"So are you saying someone else has stepped in taking over Arnez's sick obsession to hold my mother hostage?"

"That's what my gut is telling me. Someone went out of their way to have these men killed and to get your mother."

"But who?" Amir wanted to know.

Supreme stood shaking his head. "I'm not sure. We know that Maya wasn't Arnez's only partner. We know he was dealing with Emory and Markell. I doubt either one of them knew about Talisa because Maya didn't. Arnez had specific roles for everyone he did business with. Whoever has Talisa now either has their own animosity against Genesis or they've taken it upon themselves to pick up whereArnez left off."

"This can't be happening. We were so close to bringing my mom home and now we're back at square one."

"Not necessarily, Amir. I guarantee you, your mother is still being held somewhere in New York. I've already had my men tracking all flights, commercial and private. Whoever has Talisa knows we're on their trail, so they're being very cautious with how they move. We just have to find them before they figure out how to make your mother disappear again," Supreme said.

"We better hurry up because the clock is ticking. I can feel her slipping away and we can't let that happen. I refuse to lose my mother again," Amir stated.

"You made it." Skylar smiled when she opened the door to let Nichelle in.

"Yes! So sorry I'm a little late, but I stopped to get you some flowers."

"I see. They're beautiful. Thank you so much." Skylar beamed.

"Those are beautiful!"

Nichelle turned to see who had chimed in. "Precious, I had no idea you would be here. It's good to see you."

"It's good to see you, too. Those really are some beautiful flowers."

"Thank you." Nichelle smiled.

"Yes, they are. I'll be right back. I'ma go to the kitchen and put them in some water," Skylar said. "Nichelle, can I get you something to drink? Lunch should be ready shortly."

"Sure, I'll take some water or juice."

"Or you can have some champagne. That's what I'm having." Precious winked.

"Sounds good." Nichelle laughed. "I'll have what she's having."

"Okay, I'll be back in a sec."

"Skylar's very pretty," Nichelle remarked to Precious after she walked off.

"Yes, she is. Her and Genesis are going to have a beautiful baby."

"I had no idea you and Skylar were friends."

"We're very close. When she first started coming to New York to see Genesis I was the only female she really knew so we started spending time together."

"I didn't realize Skylar wasn't from New York."

"No, she moved here from LA."

"To be with Genesis?" Nichelle asked.

"Yep. He put her and her son up in this beautiful condo...promised her the world. Of course that was before he found out Talisa was alive." Precious shrugged. "Now it looks as if Skylar will be raising their child solo."

"Precious, you know Genesis will want to be a part of his child's life. He would never not take care of his baby."

"Of course he will financially provide for his child. Skylar, nor the baby, will want for anything, but we both know that is not the fairytale life Skylar envisioned having for her and their child. Once Talisa comes home, do you really think she wants to be snuggling up with Genesis and another woman's baby...huh? I can't hear you," Precious taunted, putting her index finger behind her ear and leaning forward in Nichelle's direction.

Nichelle rolled her eyes, not wanting to entertain Precious's slick mouth. She hated to admit it, but Nichelle knew that Precious had a point. Talisa had been kept away from her husband for all these years, of course she wouldn't want to come home and immediately have to share him with someone else, especially not a newborn baby.

"No doubt this is a sticky situation, but it is what it is. All of them will have to make some adjustments. But right now, they have to bring Talisa home first, Genesis has to beat his case, and

Skylar needs to deliver a healthy baby. Everything else will work itself out," Nichelle decided.

"You really think it will be that easy?" Skylar directed her question to Nichelle when she came back in the room, handing Nichelle a glass of champagne and refilling Precious's glass.

"I'm sorry. I didn't realize you heard what I said. I was talking to Precious," Nichelle explained, ready for another drink before even finishing the first.

"No need to apologize, you're simply sharing your thoughts about the situation. One thing you are right about is that we will all have to make some adjustments," Skylar agreed.

"You're hardly even showing, Skylar. How far along are you?" Nichelle asked casually observing the leggings and fitted shirt Skylar was wearing. She caught Precious cut her eyes at her and quickly grasped how inappropriate her question sounded.

"I'm still in my first trimester. Are you insinuating that I'm not really pregnant?" Skylar frowned.

Nichelle reached over on the table and grabbed the bottle of champagne, pouring herself another drink. She was now dreading her decision to come over and visit Skylar, but didn't have the nerve to get up and bolt.

"Skylar, I keep putting my foot in my mouth and once again I'm sorry. I know you must be sick of hearing those two words because I'm most def sick of saying them. That really came out wrong," Nichelle admitted.

"No need to apologize, Nichelle. I had my suspicions about the legitimacy of Skylar's pregnancy. We all know I don't bite my tongue. I mean putting a baby off on a man to try and salvage a relationship is the oldest trick in the book. But Skylar is pregnant. She even had me go to her last OB/GYN appointment to erase any doubts I might have." Precious winked.

"The difference is, Precious is my friend. I expect for her to keep it one hundred. But I don't know you like that, Nichelle."

"Now she does have a point," Precious chimed in.

"You called me and basically invited yourself over. I'm starting to feel that Genesis put you up to this so you could spy on me. See if I was telling the truth about carrying his child. I think maybe you need to go," Skylar shouted standing up.

"Skylar, no, it was nothing like that! I swear. Genesis did ask me to reach out to you, not to spy, but to make sure you and the baby were okay. He was really concerned," Nichelle said sincerely."He told me the last time you all spoke it didn't end well and you weren't taking his calls. He's worried about you and the baby. Please, let's have a do-over." Nichelle glanced over at Precious with pleading eyes to help her cause.

At first Precious took another sip of her champagne, ignoring Nichelle's obvious attempt to make her an advocate of her cause. Although she was denying it, Precious did feel Nichelle was tying to be low key shady questioning how far along Skylar was and that she wasn't showing. She had nothing against Nichelle, but Precious could care less if Skylar let her stay or threw her ass out, so she had no desire to come to her defense. But then Precious thought about Genesis. A man she had a great deal of respect for and considered a friend and what he would want.

"Skylar, I'm sure Nichelledidn't mean any harm with her comment. It just came out wrong. Poor girl probably doesn't know how to act when she gets a little liquor in her system," Precious joked with a touch of sarcasm.

"Maybe you're right." Skylar sighed, calming down. "I apologize for overreacting," Skylar said sitting back down.

"No need to apologize. If anything I'm sorry. I really want us to be friends Skylar. I'm looking forward to being an aunt. I never had that sort of relationship with Amir because there wasn't this huge age difference. We were more like friends than anything else. It'll be different with your baby...I mean if you let me," Nichelle said.

"I would like that, Nichelle. I don't have any sisters and although Precious has agreed to be the Godmother she's not really the diaper-changing, babysitting type." They all laughed.

"Can't argue with that." Precious giggled.

"I would love to babysit and change diapers," Nichelle said proudly.

"Great because I will surely need the extra help." Skylar smiled.

The three women spent the remainder of the afternoon eating, talking, and drinking, except for Skylar of course. Having Precious and Nichelle there was exactly what she needed. She was happy that she let Nichelle stay because although Skylar wanted to appear strong she was actually petrified. After having her son as a single mother, Skylar always imagined that with her second child she would be happily married and she would raise the baby with her husband. Although this time around she wouldn't be struggling financially, she would once again have to do it alone. So if Nichelle wanted to lend a helping hand, Skylar welcomed it.

Chapter Fifteen

Vanished

My man, Renny! So good to see you." T-Roc grinned as both men sat down for dinner at an upscale restaurant in downtown Philly.

"It's been too long. When Nichelle told me you were in Philly, you know I had to hit you up."

"No doubt. How is your beautiful wife doing?"

"She's good. I'm missing her like crazy. Can't wait to finish things up here so I can go be with her in New York."

"I feel you. Nichelle was always a sweet girl. She was so young when I hired her to be the spokes model for a new product my company was launching. I always felt like that was divine intervention because at the launch party is when she met Genesisfor the very first time, who of course turned out to be her brother."

"I know, that shit is so crazy. But I believe to this day, that's probably the happiest moment of her life. She still gets teary-eyed every time she tells the story," Rennysaid becoming sentimental.

"Yeah, the same for Genesis. He adores Nichelle and is so protective of her, almost like a father figure. He didn't even want her to know he was locked up."

"I know. He won't even let her come visit him in jail. They've spoken on the phone several times, but Genesis doesn't want her to see him like that. She insists on staying in New York, hoping he'll change his mind. My wife is sweet, but she can also be very stubborn." Renny chuckled.

"Well Nichelle might not have to wait too much longer if we're able to get rid of this problem," T-Roc revealed.

"Is that right?"

"Yeah. I'm almost positive we know who the

informant is on Genesis's case. If we can get rid of him, then the Fed's entire case with crumble."

"We both know how this street game go. If you gonna make a move you better do it fast."

"I'm with you. I just have to speak to one more person to get that final confirmation and then we'll strike. We might only get one shot and I wanna make sure we shooting at the right target," T-Roc stated.

"True, but you know if you need any help, I got you." Renny nodded before becoming distracted when he saw a familiar face. "Small world."

"Who you see?" T-Roc questioned not wanting to turn around and look in case Renny wanted to be discreet.

"Delondo. He's over there having dinner. Let me go over there and say hello. You wanna come with me?" Renny asked T-Roc.

"Definitely. I haven't seen him in a minute." The two men got up and went over to Delondo's table. As if feeling someone walking up on him, Delondo looked up and locked eyes with the men as they approached.

"If it ain't Renny and T-Rock. What ya doing in my city!" Delondo gave the men a wide smile, standing up and walking over giving each a hug. "I ain't seen the two of you in forever. I see you both still think you some pretty motherfuckers," Delondo joked.

Some of the patrons in the restaurant were turning around to get a look at the three very good-looking, well-dressed black men. They were holding court in the predominantly white restaurant, carrying on as if nobody else was there but them.

"Whatever, don't get mad over our swag," T-Roc joked back.

"Come over here for a second and meet my beautiful wife," Delondo said proudly. "Astrid, I wannaintroduce you to Renny and T-Roc. Some friends of mine that I haven't seen in years."

"It's a pleasure to meet you both," Astrid gave a warm smile to both men and they returned the gesture.

"So how long will you all be in town? You need to come by the house and have some drinks or we can go out for drinks," Delondo suggested.

"I would love that man, but this is a short trip," Renny said looking over at T-Roc.

"Yeah, but let's definitely meet up soon. We'll have to come back to Philly or maybe you can bring yo' ass back to New York. Don't act like that's not where you from, nigga." T-Roc laughed.

"Nah, you know I love that city. That's where it all started for me. But we gotta make that happen and I ain'ttalkin' bout some years neither... like soon," Delondo said.

"No doubt and we will."

"Renny, yo' full of shit ass. Put yo' number in my phone so I can track you down before you get missing again," Delondo said handing him his cell.

"Whatever, you the one always changing your number," Renny shot back as he put his digits in Delondo's phone. "But you get back to dinner with your wife. It was good to meet you, Astrid," Renny said handing him back his phone.

"We'll talk to you soon, Delondo, and it was good meeting you, Astrid," T-Roc added before they walked back to their table.

"I can't believe I ran into them," Delondo said to his wife, still smiling. "Renny used to be my nigga. He was a cool cat. For the longest time I didn't even realize he was cousins wit' this nigga I couldn't stand. By the time I found out, we were so tight I didn't even care."

"Wow, that's crazy. Why didn't you like his cousin?"

"Because that nigga was the devil. He did everything he could to destroy me all because he couldn't beat me in this game. The mothefucker even tried to kill me. I still got the bullet wound. But fuck 'em. He's dead now and I'm living good with my beautiful wife so it all worked out," Delondo boasted, feeling good about having his old friend Renny back in his life.

Theron, Capo, Lex, and Harvey were having drinks at a corner bar they frequented on a regular. It was in the cut, but a spot the men had frequented for years going back to when they were broke and struggling in the hoods of Philadelphia. Now the men were rich and could afford to drink anywhere they pleased, but this particular place represented a source of comfort due to the history and bond they created going there for so long. Unfortunately for them, that same history that bonded them would ultimately also tear them apart.

"So where we going next?" Capo asked as they were all heading out the front door of the bar.

"Man, we been here drinking for three fuckin' hours. The only place my ass is going is home!" Harvey popped.

"I feel you on that. I know my girl wondering why the hell I still ain't got home," Lex mumbled, barely able to walk straight.

"Ya niggas whack." Theron flung his arms. "Capo, where you wanna go? I'm down for whatever. It's still early."

"Nigga, it's two in the morning. Get the fuck outta here wit' that dumb shit. You need to take yo' ass home too. Don't nothing good happen after two in the morning other than swimming in some good pussy," Harvey shouted as all of them busted out laughing.

The men stood on the sidewalk getting a kick out of how fucked up they were. They continued to laugh and make stupid jokes oblivious to their surroundings. So when the dark-colored sedan pulled up across the now deserted street and a man walked with purpose in their direction, the group of men was taken completely off guard.

"What up, Theron!" a young dude wearing a navy blue hoodie said. It took a second for Theron to acknowledge the guy because him and his partners were still drunk laughing.

"What up. Do I know you lil' nigga?" Theron finally asked.

"Nah, but I know you and I don't fuck wit' snitches. You gotta die motherfucker," the dude said before he lit Theron up with a rapid succession of bullets. After emptying his chamber, the thug in a hoodie vanished into the dark night as quickly as he appeared.

Chapter Sixteen

Chess Moves

Astrid had stopped at a boutique to do a little shopping before picking her daughter up from preschool. She was looking for the perfect dress to wear to a Christmas party she was attending with Delondo. After looking at several places with no luck, Astrid was beginning to think she might have to get something custom made.

As Astrid left out another store and headed to her car, she felt as if someone was following her. She turned around, but didn't see anyone. Astrid still stepped up her pace feeling uneasy. When she opened her car door, Astrid froze when she felt a cold hand resting firmly on her shoulder.

"You should've known I was gonna come looking for you."

"I did, I just didn't know it would be so soon," Astrid said turning to face Renny. "Can we please not do this here. Delondo knows a lot of people. I don't want anyone to see us together.

"Let's go over to that restaurant across the street," Renny said taking Astrid's arm.

"You don't have to hold my arm. I'm not going anywhere," Astrid snapped.

"Oh, I'm making sure of that," Renny said refusing to let go.

When they got inside the restaurant the place was rather empty so the hostess seated them immediately.

"Can we get that table in the back?" Astrid asked. Of course the hostess had no problem obliging her request since there was less than a handful of people there.

"Thank you," Renny said to the hostess after they were seated. The hostess smiled and walked off leaving them alone.

"You can stop looking at me like that because I've done nothing wrong." Those were the first words out of Astrid's mouth once they sat down.

"Feeling guilty much." Renny smoothed his fingers down his thin mustache before resting it on his forehead.

"What the hell do I have to feel guilty about," Astrid spit in a defensive tone.

"Maybe you're right. Let me just call Delondo to see how he feels about being married to Arnez's sister," Renny said casually, taking out his phone.

"Don't you dare!" Astrid slammed her hand over Renny's phone trying to take it from him.

"Slow down," he said firmly holding her wrist. "Don't start something you can't finish." He then let go and Astrid placed her arm back down.

"Renny, it's not what you think," she said trying a sweeter, gentler approach.

"I had no idea you were a mind reader. By all means tell me what I think."

Astrid took a deep breath, agitated that she was being forced to explain herself to Renny. But she knew it was either that or having to answer to her husband, which wasn't an alternative.

"When I met Delondo I had no idea he ever had any dealings with Arnez. He didn't discuss his illegal activities with me. Eventually I did find out, but it didn't matter because as far as I knew Arnez was dead because you killed him."

"Interesting. So when did you find out I didn't kill Arnez and he was still alive?"

Astrid swallowed hard and shifted in her chair seeming uncomfortable. "It was a few years ago. After I was already married to Delondo. He reached out to our mother who put me in touch with him."

"You are so full of shit, Astrid. You sit there with that fake, uppity attitude you like to throw around to hide how trifling you are. You're just as bad as your brother. I'm assuming that defect in your character you and Arnez share must come from your mother's side of the family since you all have different fathers."

"Fuck you, Renny! You've always thought you were better than me."

"It wasn't that I thought I was better than you, but it was obvious even when you were a little girl, that your mother was raising you to be a con-artist just like her."

"Yet your uncle laid down and made a baby with my mother."

"Hey, we all make mistakes even my uncle. He tried to make it right. That's why Arnez lived with him. He hoped that Arnez would be more like our side of the family than yours. Unfortunately, it didn't work out that way," Renny scoffed only imagining what sort of scheming Astrid had been doing on Delondo.

"My mother did the best she could. Arnez was living over there with his daddy who had all that money while me and mother struggled in our two-bedroom apartment."

"She already couldn't afford to take care of Arnez. Nobody told her to get knocked up again by some lowlife bum and have you. That was your mother's decision. My uncle did everything he could to help her out and all she did was keep fucking up. Always lying, making up stories to get more money out of him. Then when you were old enough to talk she had you lying too. You weren't even his seed, but because you were Arnez's baby sister he looked out for you, too. But ya ungrateful asses always wanted more," Renny barked.

"Can you please keep your voice down," Astrid leaned in and said ready to explode. "I get it. You don't like me or my mother, but you don't need to announce it to everyone in the restaurant."

"Ain'tnobody here though." Renny shrugged glancing around. "You right, I don't like you or your mother so I'ma ask you one time and one time only. Your marriage to Delonodo, is Arnez's handprints on it in any way?"

"No. Arnez has nothing to do with my marriage. When we got back in touch, I did tell him about Delondo. He wasn't happy about it, but he respected the fact he was my husband. Soon after I lost contact withArnez. Then a few months ago I found out that he was dead and this time for real."

"I swear you better not be lying to me, Astrid."

"I'm not. I love my husband very much. We have a child together...a daughter. I don't think Delondo had a chance to mention that to you when he saw you at the restaurant the other night."

"No, he didn't."

"Well, now you know. Do you really want to cause unnecessary drama in our marriage when there is a young child involved?"

"I want to make sure Delondo is straight. I haven't spoken or seen him in years, but we have the sort of relationship where it doesn't matter how long we're out of touch, if we need anything, we're there for each other."

"I get that and I can assure you that I also have Delondo's back. He is the father of my child and I don't want to lose him. He's been really good to me."

"I'm sure he has. You finally found a sucker to fall for thatclassy persona you like to portray," Renny commented observing her perfectly applied makeup, freshly done manicure, silk blouse with just the right amount of cleavage, and tapered slacks. There was no denying Astrid had stepped her game all the way up."I hate it had to be my manDelondo." Renny shook his head with discontent.

"Believe it or not I've changed, Renny. I'll admit, I've made some choices that I'm not proud of, but that's in the past. I'm a wife and mother now. Don't destroy the life that I've built for myself because of your dislike for me," Astrid implored.

"Fine, I'll let you be, but don't let me find out you bullshitting me, Astrid. I left my own cousin for dead. What you think I would do to a two-bit hussy like you. My bad… a reformed two-bit hussy. You better do right by Delondo or I'm coming for you," Renny promised.

T-Roc entered Lorenzo's Greenwich Village apartment with a wicked grin spread across his face. "It's done," he bragged proudly.

"Theron is dead?" Lorenzo wanted to confirm not wanting to celebrate prematurely.

"Dead, dead. Not pretend dead, but in the morgue dead."

"You did it, man!!" Lorenzo was ecstatic. The two men gave an elbow interlock hug, patting each other on the back. "We sent the right man to get the job done. Good looking out, T-Roc."

"I couldn't let Genesis down. He always steps up to help everyone else out, I wanted to do the same for him."

"You did just that. Now with Theron dead, it'll be interesting to see what the Feds will do next," Lorenzo pondered.

"The first thing they gonna try to do is link the murder to Genesis, but they'll come up short. I made sure to make that shit clean with no traces leading to any of us. Once they realize they can't pin it on Genesis, they will then try and stall to rebuild their case some other way," T-Roc explained.

"We tryna get Genesis out. Not give the government time to build a new case," Lorenzo scoffed.

"That's why it's time for Genesis to tell his attorney he wants to request a speedy trial. That will fuck them up completely. With Theron dead they won't be prepared. But that ain't Genesis's problem. He has a right to a speedy trial and them motherfuckers will have to deal," T-Roc stated.

"I'll go see his attorney this afternoon. Let him know to file the necessary paperwork to request a speedy trial. I don't want Genesis held in jail any longer than he has to be. Meissner should have no problem getting it done."

"What are you gonna tell Meissner when he ask why you are in such a rush to get Genesis's case in front of judge and jury?"

"I ain'tgonna tell him shit, I'll let Genesis handle that. I'm simply the messenger. That's all he needs to know. Whatever the reason will be left up to Genesis to give." Lorenzo glanced down at his watch before continuing. "He should be calling me in about an hour. I'll get him prepared for what I'm about to do. That way he's prepared and ready for when his attorney shows up with a briefcase full of questions."

"And the waiting game will begin. We've made our move, let's see how the Feds react. Chess moves...all chess moves." T-Roc grinned getting an unexpected thrill at being back in the game.

Chapter Seventeen

No Escape

When Capo, Lex, and Harvey arrived at Delondo's home he didn't want to waste anytime with small talk, he just wanted facts. Even though the three men were his top lieutenants, normally Delondo would never have them at his crib, but knowing that the Feds were building a case against him, he wasn't sure who was watching or listening. The only place Delondo felt safe was in his home.

"Tell me exactly what happened and don't leave shit out," Delondo spit.

"It's like we told you," Harvey said going over the story for the third time. This was now the forth time and the story remained the same so Delondo was starting to believe it might be true.

"Boss, we were drunk, but hearing those bullets got us sober quick. What Harvey said is exactly what happened," Capo cosigned.

"Yeah, but the thing that I can't get outta my head was the shooter calling Theron a snitch. Who the fuck could Theron been snitching on? He don't get down like that," Lexsulked, feeling some type of way.

"Maybe we didn't know that nigga as well as we thought," Harvey said causing all eyes to rest on him.

"What the fuck you mean by that!" Lex shouted getting riled up. "I grew up wit' that nigga. All of us been breaking bread together for years. Now all of sudden you don't know him?! Get the fuck outta here wit' that dumb shit," Lex barked.

"Yo get mad at me if you want to. All I know is a motherfucker show up outside of a bar we been going to for years. It was four of us and he put all his bullets into one nigga. That lets me know the motherfucker wasn't on no let's wipe out Delondo's crew. He was on some let's get rid of this one foul nigga," Harvey said not backing down from his theory.

"Man, I don't wanna believe Theron was on some snitch shit, but Harvey do have a point. Won't none of us carrying weapons and we was drunk. That nigga coulda took all of us out wit' no problems, but he didn't. He killed Theron and called him out before doing so," Capo said.

Delondo had been sitting back listening to his crew go back and forth arguing with each other. Their reactions to what went down had him thinking that if Theron was the snitch, he was in it alone. None of them seemed to have any idea what he was up to. But that didn't sit well with Delondo. Most of the times when people were on some foul shit they had a partner. It was human nature to want an ally when you're up to no good. Delondo wondered though that if it wasn't Harvey, Lex, or Capo then who was Theron in cohorts with besides the Feds, of course.

"All of ya calm down," Delondo finally said becoming tired of the bickering. "Lex, I hate to break it to you, but Theron was a snitch. He was an informant with the Feds."

"What!" Harvey and Capo both said in

unison, but Lex stood dumbfounded.

"Theron was snitching to the Feds...damn!" Capo yelled out in resentment. "That nigga played me...he played all of us. We treated that motherfucker like fam, but he was a snake."

"I don't know what to say. I knew that nigga didn't walk up and kill Theron's ass for nothing, but never did I..." Harvey's voice trailed off, as he couldn't bring himself to complete his thoughts.

"That nigga was like a brother to me," Lex mumbled. He was trying to appear tough, but the pain was eating him up and everyone in the room could see it. "You coulda told me anything about that man, but never a snitch...never that. Why would he do that? I don't understand," Lex said. He was left feeling confused and wanting answers.

"Who the fuck knows why people you think are loyal and you trust fuck you over. It's one of the major downfalls of being in this game," Delondo stated. "But the damage is done. Theron might be dead, but now we're on the Feds radar."

"Is that why you haven't let us do no business for the last few weeks, Delondo, because you knew Theron was snitching?" Harvey asked.

"Yeah, but I didn't know it was Theron. I didn't know who the fuck it was. I was trying to figure that shit out so I was keeping shit low key. I was hoping it was nobody in my crew, but in my gut I knew it had to be somebody close to me or they wouldn't be of any use to the Feds," Delondo rationalized.

"Now that we know the Feds are watching us what do we do next?" Capo questioned.

"We chill. Let shit die down some more. A friend of mine is locked up right now because of Theron. I'ma wait and see what happens to his case. When things mellow out then we'll get back to business per usual," Delondo answered.

"All that sounds good, but we still got one problem," Lex said.

"What's that?" Capo asked.

"Who killed Theron? Don't we wanna know the answer to that?" Lex questioned.

"Hell nah! I know I don't give a fuck," Harvey spit.

"Neither do I. Did you not hear what the fuck I said. That nigga was an informant. He turned on us. Whoever killed him did us a favor!" Delondo roared.

"Damn sure did! Not only did Theron bring heat on us, but he's costing us money. We can't even make no moves right now because of that snitch nigga. Fuck Theron!" Capo scoffed.

Harvey was about to chime in, but when the front door opened and Astrid walked in the room went silent. Delondo wasn't expecting his wife to come back home anytime so her presence meant his meeting with the crew was over.

"Am I interrupting something?" Astrid asked feeling a tense vibe in the room.

"Of course not, baby." Delondo went over to his wife and gave her a kiss. "They were just leaving."

"Yeah, we'll get up wit' you later boss," Capo said with Harvey and Lex following his lead. Each gaveAstrid polite smiles as they passed her on the way out.

"I never took myself as a person who could clear a room," Astrid joked after Capo, Lex, and Harvey left. "I hope I didn't scare them off."

"It had nothing to do with you," Delondo said pulling his wife closer for another kiss.

"That's good to know, but what was up with all those long faces when I walked in?"

"Theron was killed last night."

"What!" Astrid was in shock. "What happened?"

"They were all coming out of a bar and someone walked up and lit his ass up," Delondo cracked.

"You don't sound too torn up about it. I thought you considered Theron to not only be a business associate but also a friend."

"I did until I found out he was the fuckin' snitch."

"Excuse me?" Astrid said as if she didn't hear Delondo correctly.

"Yeah it was that nigga who was giving up the goods to the Feds. Whoever killed that motherfucker saved me the trouble. Now hopefully Genesis can get out of jail and I can get back to business."

"I'm so glad it all worked out for you, baby." Astrid laid her head on Delondo's shoulder and gave him a hug.

"It ain't worked out yet, but with Theron out the picture more than likely it will be."

"Well I'm optimistic and you should be too. For the first time in weeks you seem to be at ease."

"That's relief you sensing. Between trynafigure out who the traitor was in my inner circle and then how to get rid of them had a nigga stressed. That burden has been lifted so I can relax a little, but not completely. There's more work to be done," Delondo confided.

"More work like what?"

"Like who the fuck Theron was working with."

"Lorenzo told you, the Feds."

"I think there's someone else. I agree with Lex on one thing. I would never take Theron as a snitch. It ain't really his style unless there was someone else pulling the strings and Theron was simply being used to make the magic happen."

"You really think Theron could be that gullible? He's a seasoned street guy, wouldn't he be the one pulling strings and not the other way around?" Astrid questioned.

"True, but I don't know. There's still a missing piece to this puzzle. I ain't gonna worry too tough about it right now. Just like Theron's skeleton got pulled out the closet, the same will happen to whomever he's working with. All I have to do is sit back and wait." Delondo nodded assertively.

"Can I get you anything?" the man who had been assigned to watch over Talisa asked as she sat on the chair watching television.

"No, I'm fine," she replied keeping her eyes glued to the monitor.

"That's fine. I'll be back in a couple hours to

bring your dinner," he said.

"When will I be going home to my family," Talisa called out before the man walked out the door.

"I'm not sure, but at this point it's looking like never."

"Why are you doing this? Arnez is dead. You don't need to keep me anymore. Please let me go home to my family," Talisa begged.

"How did you know that Arnez is dead?" the man wanted to know.

"I overheard Julio and Mario discussing it. That's why they left the island and were selling me back to my family because they no longer had any money to keep me. My family will pay for my return. Take the money and let me go."

"Someone else has taken over and unfortunately for you they have no intention of releasing you to your family. The good news is, they will make sure you live comfortably. Right now arrangements are being made for where you'll be calling home for the foreseen future."

"Does that mean you're taking me back to the island?"

"No, that's too risky. Many have now discovered what was once a private paradise. You're new home will be just as lovely though."

Talisa stared at the tall, lanky man who was handsome in an unconventional way. His presence was non-threatening and his voice was rather soothing. Never would you think he was capable of holding a woman hostage, but yet he was and it didn't seem to bother him in the least.

"So how much longer before I'm moved?" Talisa asked becoming flooded with hopelessness.

"Now that your family knows you're alive there are several people looking for you. We have to move with caution and wait until the time is right. Once it is, we'll be leaving. Until then, relax and if you need anything let me know. I want you to be comfortable." He smiled as if Talisa was voluntarily staying at a five star resort and he wanted to make her stay as perfect as possible.

Talisa's eyes darted to the large window that brought so much sunlight into her room. If the window weren't sealed closed, she would've been tempted to jump out of it to her death. After getting a little taste that freedom was within her reach, there was no way Talisa could go back to being a content prisoner no matter how beautiful the location. She didn't want to give up hope because then she would slowly begin to die.

"Amir, what's up with the long face? I just told you that my attorney went before the judge and requested a speedy trial. Unless the prosecution has another witness that we don't know about, then there's a very good chance I could get outta here. Don't tell me you gettin' used to your old man being locked up and you like it," Genesis joked.

"Never that, Dad. I'm looking forward to you coming home." Amir's words sounded optimistic, but his tone was somber.

'Tell me what's really going on, son. I'm your father. I always know when something's wrong with you. Talk to me."

Amir wavered then turned away not wanting to look his father in the eyes. "You're already going through so much. I don't want to burden you with things you have no control over," Amir conceded.

"Your burden is my burden. Tell me so we can deal with it together as father and son. Is it about your mother?" Genesis asked.

"How did you know?" Amir questioned now locking eyes with his dad.

"Because like I said, you're my son. Now tell me what's going on."

"Dad, we were so close. Supreme found the island mom had been kept on for all those years, but once he got there she was already gone. Then I got a phone call asking for money to get her back and of course I was gonna pay it. Supreme had his men in place. We were ready. I waited for hours and they never brought her. Once again Supreme found where they had been keeping her, but she was already gone. I just..." Amir stopped mid-sentence, becoming completely choked up.

"Amir, it's okay." Genesis wanted to reach over and hug his son, but knew the guards would end his visitation immediately.

"It's not okay. A mother should not be kept from her son and a son should know their mother. Why am I being denied that? It's not right."

"You're right and it's my fault."

"How is it your fault?" Amir looked confused.

"Because of the life I chose to live, my wife and my son have suffered the consequences."

"It's not your fault. It's that sick fuck Arnez who brought all this mayhem into our life. He's the evil one," Amir grumbled under his breath.

"Son, we're all born sinners. Some of us go down darker roads than others, but we still have to take responsibility for our decisions. I allowed Arnez to infiltrate our lives and all of us are paying for it."

"I know with the life we live none of us are innocent including me, but I just want to meet my mother. Is that too much to ask?"

"No, it's not. I know everyone always says that you look just like me. But when I look at you, I see your mother's eyes and her smile. You deserve to meet her and you will," Genesis said without hesitation.

Chapter Eighteen

The Walls Are Closing In

"I spoke to Genesis's attorney today. The news isn't great, but it's leaning in the right direction," Lorenzo said to T-Roc while they waited in Supreme's office for him to come back in.

"What did Meissner say?" T-Roc knew Lorenzo wanted to tell him once Supreme got back, but he couldn't wait.

"Hold on a minute. I wanna tell you both at the same time."

"Tell us both what?" Supreme questioned when he walked back in the room closing the door behind him.

Once Supreme was sitting comfortably behind his desk Lorenzo continued. "The prosecution asked the judge for more time and he granted it."

"Fuck that! Meissner requested a speedy trial and Genesis has a right to it. Just because them motherfuckers ain't got shit now, not our problem," T-Roc barked.

"True, but you know how this shit goes. The judge did throw a potential bone which is the good news."

"Tell us...what is it?" Supreme said to Lorenzo.

"He scheduled a bail hearing. Originally bail was denied, but with the prosecution needing more time and the defense being ready to move forward the judge felt this would be a happy medium."

"So while the judge gives the Feds additional time to try and build their case, he's allowing Genesis to get out and wait in the comfort of his home," Supreme surmised.

"Pretty much." Lorenzo nodded, clamping his hands together.

"I guess that's a start, but I hate the prosecution was given more time," T-Roc seethed. "But at least Genesis gets to come home. So when is the bail hearing?"

"Early next week," Lorenzo said.

"That is good news now all we have to do is bring his wife home too." Supreme let out a deep sigh. Clearly the search for Talisa was taking a toll on him.

"How is that coming?" Lorenzo asked.

"Not good. It's like every time we find her, she disappears. What's puzzling to me is who is funding this shit. It cost money to keep moving someone around from place to place. With Arnez being dead who's orchestrating this shit now?" Supreme wondered out lout.

"Who else was working with Arnez?" Lorenzo questioned.

"They're all dead as far as I know. Maya, Emory, Markell. But I did hear Markell had a woman he was seeing seriously. Supposedly he had a huge shipment of drugs that came in right before he got killed that no one was able to locate after his death," Supreme shared.

"So where you going with that?" Lorenzo

was interested to know and so was T-Roc, but for different reasons. When Supreme mentioned Markell having a woman he was seeing seriously, he couldn't help but think about the conversation he had with Jimar and his daughter Justina's name being brought up.

"What if this mystery girlfriend knew about Markell's drugs, sold them, and is using some of that money to keep Talisa hidden? She would have more than enough," Supreme reasoned.

"True, but why would this girlfriend have any interest in holding on to Talisa?" T-Roc asked.

"Yeah, I thought about that too and couldn't come up with nothing. It's just another theory yet I keep hitting a brick wall," Supreme said before being interrupted by a knock on his door. "Come in!" he called out.

"Boss, we have a lead on Talisa's whereabouts. We need to move now!" Cleavon, another one of Supreme's henchmen announced.

Supreme, Lorenzo, and T-Roc all jumped up at the same time. "I'll call Amir and tell him to meet us," Supreme said as the men headed out the door.

Talisa had just finished taking a much needed hot shower. The warm water drenching her naked body was like therapy for her soul. It was her opportunity to let her mind escape her current predicament. Talisa stared at her reflection in the mirror. While she was on the island it seemed as if time had stood still and she hadn't aged a day in her life. But now if you looked deeply into her eyes, the years of heartache and pain were beginning to surface as she began having flashbacks of her time with Genesis. From the first day they met, to the first time they made love and when they exchanged wedding vows and then being ripped out of his life. The tears were starting to build up, but Talisa had no time to shed them when the banging started on the bathroom door.

"Get dressed! We're leaving now!" she heard the man yelling. It startled Talisa because he was always so calm. She never heard him raise his voice.

"Why are we leaving so soon?" she opened the door and asked.

"Because we have to go!" he appeared agitated.

"I just got out the shower. I need to get my stuff together."

"Leave it here. I'll get you whatever you need when we get to the new place. Just put this on," he said tossing Talisa a sweat suit, "and let's go!"

He stood over Talisa letting her know that this wasn't a request and he had no intention of letting her take her sweet time. She took the hint and quickly got dressed. The man cuffed Talisa's wrist, put duct tape over her mouth, but was in such a hurry he didn't blindfold her. He then rushed her out a back elevator with a gun pointed to her lower torso the entire time until they got to a garage where he tossed her in the back seat of a tinted sedan. He was literally panicking and Talisacouldn' t figure out why until they pulled out the garage.

As he drove around the block he was rushing to turn the corner, but got cut off by another car. That's when Talisa noticed a fleet of black SUV's pull up in front of a building and what appeared to be a small army of men rushing to go inside. But there was one young man that caught her eye and she couldn't turn away. She knew without a shadow of a doubt that young man was her son, Amir. He was the spitting image of his father. It was like Talisa had gone back in time and was seeing Genesis on their last day together. In her mind she was calling out for Amir, but no words were able to come out as the car she was in sped away.

The men rushed up the stairs with Supreme leading the way. Andre had already given him the apartment number and it was easy to find because there was only one unit per floor. When they reached the destination there was no need to force their way in because the door was wide open.

"Not again!" Supreme roared stepping into the apartment.

"They didn't even have time to turn off the television," Lorenzo commented as they walked through the massive apartment.

"This must have been where my mother was," Amir said seeing a robe on the floor and female products on the bathroom counter. When Amir came out the bathroom he saw Supreme saying something to Cleavon before he rushed off.

"Everybody, follow me to the living room," Supreme ordered.

"What's going on, Supreme?" Lorenzo asked once everyone was in the same room.

Without saying a word Supreme pulled out his gun and put it to the side of Trigger's head. Cleavon then reached in the back of Trigger's pants and retrieved his weapon in case he got any ideas.

"Yo, Supreme, what you doing?!" Lorenzo's eyes widened in confusion.

"What the fuck it look like he doing?" T-Roc shrugged. "Obviously that nigga done fucked up."

"Boss, w-what's going on?" Trigger stuttered.

"It ain't no coincidence we keep being one step behind whoever it is that has Talisa. Somehow, someway they always manage to break out before we get here. I'm tired of this shit."

"Boss, I get that. I'm tired of this shit too, but that ain't got nothing to do wit' me," Trigger said nervously.

"Nigga, you a lie. When that call came in from my investigator, Cleavon said the only person he told was you. Cleavon, get his phone. Tell him the passcode," he said to Trigger, which he reluctantly gave.

"Look at this, boss," Cleavon said giving Supreme Trigger's phone.

Supreme looked at the call log and then the text messages. "So you called this number right after you got the info about Talisa's whereabouts. Then right after you sent this text saying on the way. What type of bullshit is this?" Supreme jammed the barrel of his gun into Trigger's head.

"It's not what you think, Supreme," Trigger said nervously before he started rambling making no sense.

"I'ma ask you one motherfuckin' time. Who are you working with and where did they take Talisa?"

"I swear, Supreme I don't know. I only had contact with a dude named Fulton. He was the one I was supposed to call anytime we were about to make a move."

"How did he pay you? Cause I know you wasn't doing this shit for free." Supreme was becoming angrier by the second.

"I had a P.O. Box. He would leave the money in there and I would pick it up. I only met with him one time in person. It was easy money and he promised they were taking good care of Talisa and she wasn't hurt," Trigger said. "Boss, I had a bad gambling habit and I owed so much money. They promised me she was okay," Trigger continued, trying to justify his bullshit.

"You sorry sonofabitch! You sold my mother out to pay off your gambling debts. Fuck you!" Amir said lunging forward, ready to rip Trigger's head off.

"We got this," Lorenzo said holding Amir back.

"We damn sure do," Supreme said evenly, pulling the trigger as Trigger's brain matter marked the taupe-colored wall. "Clean this shit up," Supreme said to his men as he stepped over Trigger's dead body that lay motionless on the hardwood floor.

"What's next?" T-Roc asked ready to go.

"Let's find out everything we can about this Fulton nigga. Starting with his number although I'm sure it's a burner phone," Supreme said calling the number from Trigger's cell, but not getting an answer. "He probably already tossed it. No worries, the walls are closing in. They're running out of places to hide," Supreme said as they exited out the building more determined than ever to bring Talisa home before Genesis got out.

Chapter Nineteen

Good vs. Evil

"Damn baby, it feels so good to be back inside of you," Renny moaned going deeper and deeper with each stroke in Nichelle's inner walls. "You so wet," he whispered in her ear. "You missed me, too?."

"You know I did," Nichelle breathlessly whispered back. She gripped Renny tightly, enthralling every inch of her body to his. As he lifted his upper body staring intensely into Nichelle's eyes, he slowed down his pace and took his time so she could feel every inch and width. Nichelle wanted to scream out from the pleasure and the pain, but instead she began biting down then kissing and licking up and down Renny's strong muscular arms.

Renny could've made love to his wife all night long as the heat their bodies generated made them feel like one. And while his mind was lost in staying inside of his wife's warmth forever, Nichelle prayed that she and her husband's love making had created the child she yearned for.

"Come back to bed," Nichelle whined looking over at the clock to see what time it was.

"Babe, it's about to be the middle of the afternoon," Renny said as he finished getting dressed.

"I can't believe how late I slept. But then again, we did make love all night long."

"We had a lot of time to make up for." Renny smiled.

"I thought we were going to spend all day in bed," Nichelle said leaning her elbow on the pillow. "I can still smell your scent on me. Please come back to bed."

Renny came over to Nichelle, tilting over her naked body, softly kissing her exposed nipple.

"When I get back I promise to stay right by your side for the rest of the day and night."

"When are you coming back?"

"I won't be gone long. I have to meet up with T-Roc for a minute, then run a couple of errands before coming back to my beautiful wife," Renny said giving Nichelle a kiss.

"You never told me how your trip to Philly went. Clearly things went well between you and T-Roc since you're seeing him again here in New York."

"Yeah, you know I dig T-Roc. He good people. We had a nice dinner while we were in Philly. I also ran into an old friend of mine, Delondo. It was really good to see him."

"How's he doing?"

"He's doing really good. He's married now with a little girl. He's doing the whole family thing. Too bad his wife is a trifling skank," Renny scoffed putting on his shoes.

"Wow, that's harsh," Nichelle said rising up in the bed.

"It's the truth. She's Arnez's sister."

"I never knew Arnez had a sister. So she's your cousin too and you've never mentioned her."

"Astrid is not my cousin. Her and Arnez have the same mother, but not the same father. My father and Arnez's father were brothers."

"Oh, so why do you dislike her so much?" Nichelle asked.

At first Renny sat down on the edge of the bed and simply shook his head as if he didn't even want to discuss why he couldn't stand Astrid, but he knew Nichelle would keep pressing him for the answer.

"My uncle always looked out for Astrid because she was Arnez's baby sister. She had a bum ass daddy that didn't do shit for her and her mother was a con-artist slut," Renny spit.

"Then why did Arnez's father have a child with her?"

"My uncle had a good heart and when it came to hustling he was great at it. But when it came to women he was a sucker for a pretty face and nice body. Laying with that chick that handful of times was one of the worst mistakes he ever made.

When Arnez was about nine he started living with his dad full time because all his mother wanted to do was run the streets even though she had two small kids at home. In a lot of ways Arnez's dad acted like a father to Astrid too. If he did for Arnez, he did for her."

"I think that's sweet. I'm sure she appreciated it," Nichelle said.

"Maybe she would've if her mother hadn't started corrupting her mind at such an early age. After all my uncle did for her, when she was like fourteen she accused my uncle of rape."

"What!" Nichelle's eyes widened, as that was the last thing she expected Renny to say.

"She sure did. I always knew she was no good. Astrid was always scheming, asking my uncle to give her money for this or for that. She would even come to my dad with a sad story so he would give her some money. She learned all that bullshit from her mother. My uncle was still helping her out even after Arnez started living with him full time. They wasn't dealing with each other on no personal level, but she was the mother of his son and she had another child and he felt bad for her. But eventually he wised up and cut her off. That's when she and Astrid came up with her master plan to bring my uncle down."

"Are you saying Arnez's mother and sister plotted together?"

"Damn right. One day when her ass was supposed to be in school she showed up at my uncle's house and her young, scandalous ass tried to throw him some pussy. He hurried up and got her out his house. The next day the police showed up at his house and arrested him for rape against a minor," Renny huffed shaking his head.

"That's horrible! Did he end up doing time?"

"He would've. But like I said he was dumb when it came to a pretty face, but he was smart when it came to handling business. Arnez's mother actually had the nerve to call him, tryna shake my uncle down for money. Saying Astrid wouldn't testify against him in court if he gave her and her daughter some money for their troubles."

"So your uncle had to pay them off so he wouldn't go to jail on some bogus rape charges?" Nichelle asked in disgust at what she was hearing.

"That's what they were hoping for... a nice payday. They dumb asses didn't know my uncle kept cameras all in his house because he moved a lot of weight back in the day so it made him a target. He had the entire incident on tape. When his lawyer turned it over to the prosecution they dropped that case so quick. "

"Thank goodness! That was a smart move on your uncle's part," Nichelle agreed.

"Yeah, but if he didn't have those cameras, he could've spent years in jail on some trumped up charges."

"That's crazy. I guess that pretty much ruined Arnez's relationship with his sister."

"Just the opposite."

"Huh?!"

"Yep. Arnez was a fucked up nigga, but he had a real soft spot for his sister. After that shit happened he tried to make excuses for her ratchet ass, but my uncle wasn't having it. He would not allow her back in his house. By that time Arnez had started hustling. He was going to see his mother and sister behind his dad's back, giving them money and shit. He didn't want any problems with his father so he kept it on the low. You would've thought the situation with my uncle would get Astrid's mind right, but nope. She continued on, setting up niggas doing all sorts of heinous shit and this is the chick my homeboy ended up marrying." Nichelle could hear the frustration in Renny's voice.

"In fairness, that was years ago. Maybe she's changed."

"So she says. That's the only reason I didn't go to Delondo. He doesn't even know that she's Arnez's sister."

"Why would that matter?"

"Delondo and Arnez were enemies. He's probably right under Genesis in terms of niggas Arnez hates list."

"Are you serious. So Astrid had no idea that

her brother and husband were enemies?"

"That's the story Astrid running with. She claims she didn't find out until after her and Delondo were already married."

"But you don't believe her?"

"Hell no! I don't believe that chick even understands the concept of telling the truth."

"Then why don't you tell your friend what you know? At least he'll have all the facts."

"Because they share a young child together. As much as I dislike Astrid I could be wrong. If she really has changed, I don't wanna be the reason a family is left in shambles."

"I understand." Nichelle went over and wrapped her arms around the back of Renny's shoulders. "Still, I know it must be hard for you to keep this information to yourself."

"You have no idea. Astrid is nothing nice. For Delondo's sake, I pray she's a changed woman." Renny sighed.

Skylar was driving through an exclusive neighborhood in Alpine, NJ looking at multimillion dollar homes. She was envisioning living in one of the lavish homes with her son and unborn child.

She decided that she no longer wanted to live in the heart of New York City, but instead, wanted to raise her children in the suburbs. Although she would love for Genesis to live there with her and the kids, Skylar knew that was wishful thinking. Once Talisa was found and brought home her dream of a happily ever after with the man she loved was over.

"Ohmigosh! That house is stunning!" Skylar beamed stopping in front of a massive home that resembled an opulent French Estate. "Could you imagine growing up here, my little sweet baby," she cooed rubbing her now protruding belly.

Skylar continued to ogle the home for a few more minutes before continuing her ride down the street. "That's a beautiful house, too," she commented out loud glancing over to the other side of the tree-lined street. As Skylar was about to turn around and drive back up the street so she could get a better look at the house she damn near ran into a mailbox when she saw a face from her past. She quickly turned away not wanting the man to recognize her. But he seemed distracted so Skylar figured he didn't notice her in the car though she definitely noticed him.

"What in the hell is he doing here?!" she cried out loud. At first Skylar was going to keep going straight, wanting to leave the man in her past, but curiosity got the best of her. She wanted to be discreet and luckily another car had come down the street so it was a perfect opportunity for her to get behind that car and follow the man from a distance.

A few seconds later, he made a right turn and Skylar stayed back to see how far down the street he went. When she saw he was pulling into a driveway, she then turned right down the street too and parked a few feet away to see what he was doing.

The man pulled into the four car garage, but hadn't closed it. Skylar noticed the tall man get out of the dark sedan and open the back car door. Skylar's heart dropped when she saw him pulling Talisa out of the backseat. She didn't know his name, but she recognized his face from the island. He would come check on them frequently, but never spoke a word to her or Talisa directly. Now he was here in New Jersey and he had Genesis's wife.

"I need to call Supreme and let him know where Talisa is," Skylar mumbled nervously. She fidgeted with her phone about to dial Supreme's number, but she stopped. She remained stagnant as her evil versus good voice battled it out. The evil voice won. Skylar pressed down on the gas and drove away.

Chapter Twenty

Welcome Home

"Surprise!" Everyone yelled when Amir and Genesis walked through the door.

"Normally I hate surprises, but man I'm so happy to see all of you." Genesis smiled.

"We're so happy you're home," Precious said giving Genesis a hug. "Aaliyah and Nico wanted to come, but she's in the midst of planning her wedding and Nico is in Miami trying to make up for lost time with his daughter Angel, but they both send their best. Plus, I'm sure Nico will be blowing up your phone soon.

"I'm really happy for Nico. He's been searching for his daughter for so long. I'm glad they finally reunited."

"So you knew about Angel... for how long?"

"At least a year now," Genesis revealed.

"You knew all that time and never told me?"

"Precious, you know it wasn't my place to disclose Nico's personal business. I had to respect his privacy as I've done for you in the past."

Precious knew exactly what Genesis was referring to. When she was carrying on in an illicit affair with Lorenzo, not once did Genesis divulge her secret. "Point taken. Enough about that... welcome home." She smiled.

"Man, I'm so happy to see you out of that bullshit orange attire they had you wearing," T-Roc joked.

"I didn't get to see you in the orange gear, but I'm so happy you're home!" Nichelle hugged her brother tightly.

"It's so good to see my baby sister. Thank you for staying in New York and waiting for me to get out and come home."

"I wasn't leaving until I did." Nichelle and Genesis continued to embrace as if making up for all the time they had spent apart.

While everyone was in Genesis's face, happy to see him finally free at least for the time being, Precious noticed the one person she had no interest in talking to making a beeline in her direction. She wanted to make a run for it but there was nowhere to hide. So Precious stood with her arms folded and a grimaced face hoping that would make Chantal go in the opposite direction, but it didn't work.

"Precious, I've been meaning to call you."

"How? You don't have my number."

"You know that's simply a minor oversight. "

"Chantal, what do you want?" Precious asked not wanting to engage in small talk with the queen of crazy.

"I never had an opportunity to formally apologize for what I put you and your family through. You, and especially Aaliyah, didn't deserve any of it."

"Tell me something I don't already know," Precious mocked. "All that time you spent in the loony bin and that's the best you got. They didn't seem to teach you much or maybe you're a slow learner."

"No need to be nasty," Chantal hissed.

"I haven't shown you nasty, Chantal, and

trust me, you don't want to see it."

"This attitude of yours isn't helping anything. Our daughters are best friends. They're like sisters. Justina is going to be the maid of honor in Aaliyah's wedding. The two of them are closer than ever. We really need to put what happened in the past behind us and move on. If not for our sake then our kids."

"Last I checked, Aaliyah is a grown woman. I have no control over the company she keeps, including your daughter. I still haven't figured out if Justina is genuinely a sweet girl who made a mistake because she wanted to protect her mother. Or if she's faking it and your daughter is just like you. So no, we'll never be one big happy family. This ain't the Brady Bunch and I ain't Carol Brady."

"Must you be so low class, Precious. I mean you were married to Supreme, Didn't you learn anything from being his wife."

"Yes, I did. I learned there were much better ways to destroy your enemy besides just putting your foot up their ass." Precious gave Chantal a devious chuckle.

"What is that supposed to mean?" Chantal questioned putting her hand on her hip and pouting her lips.

"It means if you ever cross me or my daughter again, T-Roc will not be able to save you. There won't be no sending you off to some plush resort camouflaged as a mental facility. You'll be dealing with me and you'll see just how nasty I can be."

"I guess it's true what they say. You can take the girl out the projects and put her in a penthouse suite, but she's still just a Brooklyn hoodrat."

"So says the ran-through industry hoe from the Chi-town gutter. Humph. But you're right. I'll always be that bitch from the Brooklyn projects and I wouldn't have it any other way. So you remember that next time you're sitting around plotting on me, or anyone in my motherfuckin' family. Now move the hell out my way," Precious popped, brushing past Chantal.

"Is everything alright over here?" T-Roc asked Chantal after he passed Precious as she was walking away. "Precious seemed a little agitated."

"You know how she is. I was trying to make nice since our daughters are best friends, but Precious was being her typical bitchy self," Chantal huffed, grabbing the champagne glass out of T-Roc's hand and gulping it down. "That woman totally works my nerve."

"Chantal relax. You know it's not healthy for you to get yourself worked up."

"Would you please not talk to me like I'm your patient. You know how I hate that," Chantal snapped. "I need another drink."

"No, I think we need to go home."

"But we haven't even been here that long."

"It's been long enough. Come on, let's go," T-Roc said taking his wife's hand and leading her out the door.

"I wonder why T-Roc is leaving so soon," Supreme commented to Precious as they watched the couple leave.

"Chantal is probably off her meds. T-Roc is doing all of us a favor by escorting her out."

"Be nice."

"Listen, that woman is truly coocoo or she's a cold piece of work. Either way, I don't trust her or her daughter."

"You don't trust Justina?" Supreme raised an eyebrow. "Why... she saved Aaliyah's life and yours too. I'm sure you haven't forgotten that."

"Of course not and I'm grateful to Justina for that. It's probably the only reason I can truly forgive her for what she put Aaliyah through. But it doesn't mean I trust her. I mean look who her mother is. You can't escape that sort of DNA unscathed."

"Speaking of DNA, how is Skylar and the baby doing? She's getting up there in months."

"How did my comment about DNA make you think of Skylar and her unborn child? Are you trying to insinuate that Genesis should get a DNA test because the baby might not be his?"

"No, you're thinking too hard unless you have your doubts about the paternity," Supreme probed.

"I'll admit I had my doubts about her being pregnant at first, but I do believe Genesis is the father of the baby Skylar is carrying. I know I'm in the minority, but I wish Skylar and Genesis could raise the child together as a family. I know how much she loves him and I think deep down he loves her more than he wants to admit."

"You might end up getting what you want because if we can't find Talisa soon, I don't know if we ever will." Supreme sighed.

"You all haven't made any progress since finding that apartment she was being held at in the city?"

"None."

"That was weeks ago."

"I know. I was praying we would've found her before Genesis got out, especially after his release was pushed back. But all our leads have dried up. I'm afraid they found a way to get Talisa back out of the country. If so, it will be damn near impossible for us to get her back."

Precious hated to see the defeat and distress on Supreme's face. "I wanted Skylar and Genesis to stay together, but not at Talisa's expense. I can only imagine what that poor woman has been through. Then Genesis and Amir who has never even met his mother. So sad," Precious said putting her head down.

"I know they've all been through so much. It will take a miracle to make it right," he declared to Precious. He refused to say it out loud, but with each passing day, Supreme felt that miracle was becoming further out of reach.

Chapter Twenty-One

Atonement

"Wow, look at you! You're glowing and that belly growing," Precious said full of excitement when Skylar sat down at the table where they met for lunch.

"Can you believe it? It's like overnight I went from a flat stomach to this round pouch. I love it though. It makes this pregnancy feel so real." Skylar smiled.

"I know what you mean. When I was pregnant

with Xavier it seemed like it took forever for me to start showing. I started panicking like am I really pregnant. Then one day out the blue my stomach just blew up. I was thrilled. I desperately wanted to give Supreme a child of his own. I knew he loved Aaliyah like she was his, but I never wanted him to feel as if I shared this amazing gift with Nico, but not with him. If that makes any sense," Precious said.

"It makes perfect sense. When you're in love with someone, having a child is the ultimate bond. As much as you and Supreme love each other, it's only natural you would want to share that together."

"I'm sure you want it to be that way with Genesis too."

"I do. but I don't think it's going to happen," Skylar said sadly.

"Have you spoken to him?"

"No. He's called me a few times, but what is there really left to say."

"I'm sure you know he's out on bail."

"Yeah, he called and left me a message and also sent me a text. He just wanted to see if I needed anything. The problem is what I need he can't give me... him. Have you seen him since he's gotten out?"

"Yes. Amir put together a little welcome home party at the last minute to surprise him. He looked good and relieved to be out. Hopefully he'll end up being out permanently."

"I hope so, too. My baby needs their father," Skylar said looking down at her stomach and rubbing it. "I've made so many bad choices. I only pray my baby doesn't suffer for my sins."

"Skylar, why would you say something like that? Don't be so hard on yourself. I'm not the Bible-toting type, but let me just take it there for one second. When I was a little girl I never forgot what Mrs. Duncan, a lady who would take care of me used to say. None of us will ever be worthy, it's only because of His grace. We're all flawed, Skylar, some more than others. But your baby will be perfect because he or she was created with love."

"I want to believe that, but I've done such horrible things. I never should've left Talisa on that island," Skylar cried, shaking her head back and forth. "Genesis will never forgive me."

"I'm not condoning what you did because it was wrong... very wrong, but I do understand. Sometimes we do the craziest things in the name of love. But if it makes you feel any better, I doubt Genesis will ever find out," Precious said.

"Why do you think that?"

"I'm not gonna tell him and you're not gonna tell him. The only other person that would know is Talisa. From what Supreme told me, they don't think they're going to find her. All the leads have dried up. That happy reunion between Genesis and Talisa will probably never happen," Precious divulged.

"Oh gosh! I think I'm gonna be sick." Skylar then burst into tears and Precious assumed her hormones were on overdrive, but that had nothing to do with it. Skylar's guilty conscious had her on edge.

"Here, have some water," Precious offered, handing her a glass. Skylar drank it all down not stopping once. "I know pregnancy can make you super sensitive because your emotions are all over the place, but you really have to relax, Skylar. Getting yourself all worked up can't be good for you or the baby."

"I love him so much, you know," Skylar muttered through tears. All I wanted was for us to be happy... be a family. But not like this," she continued to wail.

"Not like what? Skylar, you're not making any sense. Help me understand where all this is coming from." Precious was trying to be a good friend, but Skylar's behavior had her baffled.

"I'm sorry, Precious, but I have to go." Skylar hopped up and grabbed her purse. "I'll call you later."

"Skylar, come back!" Precious called out, but she was gone. "She sure moves fast for a pregnant girl." Precious shrugged before calling the waitress over to order something to eat.

Skylar debated with herself the entire drive over, even as she rode up the elevator, all the way until she knocked on the door and she still hadn't made up her mind.

"I was so surprised when the doorman said you were on your way up," Genesis said when he opened the door. "You haven't returned any of my phone calls. It's so good to see you. Please come in."

"How are you?"

"Much better now that I'm home and you're here. You look beautiful!" Genesis exclaimed amazed at her protruding belly in the crimson red wrap dress she was wearing. "I wasn't expecting you to be showing as much as you are. Can I put my hand there?" Genesis asked, motioning towards her stomach.

"Sure." Skylar was surprised by his request. Genesis laid his hand on her stomach and this huge smile crept across his face. Just like that, once again Skylar had changed her mind about telling Genesis the truth. Seeing how delighted he appeared about the pregnancy, got Skylar fantasizing about what a happy family they could be if only Talisa was out of the picture.

"Do you know if it's a girl or a boy?" Genesis asked.

"Yes, I'm having a little girl," Skylar beamed. "Although the most important thing was having a healthy baby, I was secretly hoping for a little girl."

"I can't believe I'ma have a daughter. My little girl." Genesis grinned. "She's going to be so tired of her old man. I'm not going to let her move out the house until she's at least twenty-five." He laughed.

"I know what you mean. I'm sure I'll be super protective of her, too."

"Come sit down. Can I get you something to drink or are you hungry? I can have the concierge order whatever you like."

"I'm fine," Skylar said sitting down. "I wasn't expecting you to be so kind to me."

"Why wouldn't I be? I know the last time we

talked the conversation didn't end well. It really bothered me and I thought about what I said and I'm sorry for being insensitive to your feelings."

"Genesis, you don't have to apologize. You were being honest and I can't be mad at you for that."

"The thing is I was scared. I didn't want to admit it at the time, but I was locked up and I didn't think I was gonna get out. I still don't know what's gonna happen, but now that I'm home I feel stronger and more optimistic about the situation. Then when I see you. You're so beautiful and carrying my child... my daughter, it makes me want to fight harder to maintain my freedom." Genesis's words were so heartfelt that it moved Skylar.

"Thank you for saying that," Skylar said as her eyes began to water up.

"Why are you crying?" Genesis came over and sat next to Skylar. He felt so drawn to her even more than usual. He wasn't sure if it was because she was pregnant with his child or because he hadn't seen her or been with a woman in so long because he had been locked up. Or maybe it was a combination of both. All Genesis knew was that at that very moment he wanted to make love to Skylar.

"I've been doing a lot of that today."

Genesis took his hand and wiped away the tear coming down her cheek. He then leaned in and began kissing her. For Skylar it was like the sweetest kiss she had ever known. Their kisses became more intense and passionate.

"Wait!" Skylar moved back, releasing herself from Genesis's embrace. "Do you want me because you're afraid that you won't get Talisa back?"

"Skylar, why are you doing this? You know that I love you."

"But you love Talisa more and if she walked through that door right now you would choose her."

"Let's not talk about the ifs. We need to talk about us," Genesis suggested.

"I can't do this," Skylar jumped off the couch and cried becoming hysterical. She could see the fear in Genesis's eyes because he had no clue what was wrong with her.

"Skylar, you need to calm down. I had no idea this Talisa situation was taking such a toll on you emotionally. This isn't healthy for you. I'm so sorry, baby. Never did I mean to hurt you. Please come sit down."

"I can't sit down."

"Why?"

"Because when I'm next to you and you're so loving I want to forget about the wrong I've done and pretend that I can have the fairytale life I dreamed of having with you. But I know that's not possible." Skylar broke down crying again.

"Forget what wrong? Whatever it is we can get through it."

"No, we can't. You're going to hate me for this, but I won't be able to look myself in the mirror another day if I don't tell you the truth."

"Tell me the truth about what?" Genesis was now standing up, insisting that Skylar tell him what the hell was going on. "Talk to me, Skylar!"

"I was on that island with Talisa. I left her there," Skylar blurted out.

"What?" his voice was almost inaudible. "But you said..."

"I know what I said, but it was all lies. When I woke up on that island she was there. I had no clue she was Talisa, the love of your life. But we got to talking and she said all she wanted to do was get back to her husband, Genesis, and her son. My heart dropped."

"Talisa could be home right now." Genesis shook his head, his face full of anguish.

"I know and I feel horrible. I was about to

tell you the truth the day the Feds came and arrested you. Then I found out I was pregnant and I couldn't imagine my life without you in it. I know I'm a horrible person and I hate myself for what I did."

"So why are you telling me this now, Skylar? When it looks like you're gonna get what you want. I'm sure Precious told you that Talisa has basically vanished and we have no new leads. I think I would've preferred you keep this secret to yourself since there is nothing I can do about it now, but get pissed the fuck off," Genesis said angrily.

"The reason why I'm telling you now is because I've been given another opportunity to atone for my sins, right my wrong and I almost blew it again," Skylar admitted becoming choked up.

"What are you saying?"

"A few weeks ago by some crazy coincidence I saw her."

"A few weeks ago!" Genesis barked unable to contain his anger. "You saw her a few weeks ago and you're just now telling me! They've probably moved her again by now. What the fuck is wrong with you!" he roared.

"No, she's still there," Skylar said calmly.

"How do you know?"

"Because everyday I've been driving by there. It was the only way I could sleep at night." Skylar then reached in her purse. "Here is the address and a picture of the house. I think there is only one or maybe two men staying there, at least that's all I've seen."

Genesis took the piece of paper with the address and the picture of the house. He scrutinized the image and then glanced up at Skylar. He wasn't sure what to say. His emotions were mixed. So instead of saying something he might regret, Genesis chose not to speak on it all for the time being.

"I have to go," he finally said.

"Of course. I can see myself out." Once Skylar left Genesis's penthouse, she stood outside his door and let the tears flow. "I've lost him forever," Skylar cried before walking away.

Chapter Twenty-Two

At Last

Genesis and his crew pulled up to the all-brick colonial home on Bristol Ct. in Alpine, NJ just as the sun went down and nightfall set in. It was a sneak attack and they were more than prepared, in case Skylar had it wrong in terms of how many men were on the premises. At first they observed the house from a distance to see if there was any suspicious activity taking place. But the house was perfectly quiet just like the neighborhood.

Once they decided it was a go, they secured the perimeter before gaining entry into the house.

They descended into the house like a S.W.A.T. team. Fulton didn't even have a chance to retrieve his weapon. By the time he heard the chaos and realized what was going on, he was staring down the barrel of multiple guns.

"Where is she?" Genesis stepped forward and asked. The spacious house had to be at least six thousand square feet and Genesis didn't want to waste any time going room to room searching for Talisa only to realize she wasn't there.

"Where is who?" Fulton replied, pretending to have no idea what Genesis was talking about.

Making it clear he was playing no games, Genesis grabbed the gun from one of his men and swung it across the bridge of Fulton's nose breaking it. Fulton howled out in pain, holding on to his nose as blood squirted everywhere, covering his hands and dripping through his fingers. But Genesis didn't stop there. He flung the tall, lanky man down on the hardwood floor shoving his black Kinetic Gore-tex boot in his throat.

"Where is my wife?" Genesis could see the man was struggling to try and say something so he eased up his boot from off his neck.

"She's in the bedroom at the very end of the hall. You'll need this to get in," Fulton said, reaching in his back pocket for the key.

Genesis grabbed the key and rushed up the stairs. He needed to grill the man and find out who he was working for, but his desire to find Talisa and make sure she was okay outweighed that need. When Genesis got to the top of the stairs the hallway was so long that the bedroom door seemed like it was on the other side of the world. But Genesis didn't walk, he ran to open that door and his heart was beating rapidly the entire time. The reason was that he feared once opened, there would be no Talisa behind the door just another dead end. When Genesis put the key in the lock he prepared himself for the disappointment he had quickly grown accustomed to.

His heart sank when he entered the bedroom and it was empty. There was a light on, but no sign of his wife. He turned to walk away and go back downstairs to stump the man who sent him on a cruel goose chase. Then he heard the most beautiful voice.

"Genesis." Talisa called out with hesitation and uncertainty in her voice.

Genesis turned around slowly and saw his wife standing in the doorway of the bathroom. He didn't believe what he was seeing to be real. His eyes were playing tricks on him or so he thought. Talisa stood there in a long white nightgown. Her hair was in two long braids. It seemed as if time had stood still because she hadn't aged a bit, but as he walked closer it was the despair that lurked in her eyes that gave away all she had been through.

"My beautiful, Talisa," Genesis said softly, gently touching every feature on her face, her hair, and then taking her hand. He was struggling to accept that his wife was alive and standing right in front of him. "Is this a dream... are you real?"

"Yes. It's me, Genesis. I'm home. I'm finally home."

A tear rolled down his face and Talisa kissed it away. Without saying another word they held each other tightly. Genesis wanted to take in her scent, her touch. He could've stood there and held on to his wife for an eternity. As Talisa and Genesis stood there in silence, reconnecting their souls, it came to a sudden stop when the sound of a gunshot rang out.

"What was that?" Talisa questioned as terror kicked in. She didn't want her happy reunion to be cut short due to more mayhem.

"You stay here and lock the door. Don't open it until I come back. Okay?"

Talisa nodded her head yes. As soon as Genesis made his exit she locked the door, praying he would return soon. He hurried to see what was going on.

"What the fuck happened?!" Genesis exhaled seeing Fulton's dead body slumped over on the chair holding a gun.

"Genesis, I didn't have a choice," one of his men said. "He asked if he could sit down and we let him. I guess he had a gun hidden over there. I caught him reaching for it so I shot him."

"Damn! I needed to find out who he was working for. Arnez is dead so that means I have another enemy out there who wants to take me down. Now that he's dead I'll never know."

During their ride back to Genesis's place he and Talisa hardly said two words to each other. Instead, they held hands and Talisa rested her head on his shoulder. They didn't need to speak, being in each other's presence was fulfilling enough.

Genesis had already sent Amir a text telling him it was important that he meet him at his house. He had made the decision not to inform his son or anyone in his inner circle about what Skylar had told him in case it ended up being a bust. He especially wanted to spare Amir from any further disappointment. Genesis could see how much of an emotional toll it was having on his son not being able to find his mother.

When they entered Genesis's place Amir was already there. At first Amir didn't see his mother because his father came in first. "Dad, what's going on? You were so vague in your text. Is everything okay... did something happen?"

"Yes, something did happen."

"What!"

"I thought it was time you met your mother." Genesis stepped to the side and for the first time Amir laid eyes on the woman that gave him life.

"My mother," he mouthed. Amir had reconciled that he would never meet his mother or have a relationship with her. Now, against all odds there she stood like an angel.

"My son. Look how handsome you are," she said feeling so proud. Talisa went to Amir and they wrapped their arms around each other. "I had never met you, yet I loved you more than anyone else in this world. You're my child," she cried.

Genesis stood off to the side and observed as mother and son united for the very first time and it was the most beautiful vision he had ever witnessed. After relishing in their happiness, Genesis walked over and joined Talisa and Amir. He had his son and his wife. They were finally a family again.

Chapter Twenty-Three

Under The Radar

"I must say I'm very proud of you," Precious said pouring Skylar another cup of tea.

"Proud of me for what? Doing what I should've done in the first place?" Skylar shrugged. "All of it is my fault."

"No, it isn't! You're not the one who held Talisa captive on some remote island for all those years. That was that crazy motherfucker, Arnez. And don't forget he dragged yo' ass their too,"

Precious snapped, reaching for her champagne. Leaving the herbal tea for Skylar to drink.

"I know that, but I should've told Genesis the truth the moment I got back to New York."

"True. That was fucked up, but you made up for it. Hell, Genesis, Talisa, and Amir should be thanking you. If it weren't for you having a conscious, Talisawould still be hauled up in that house or be stashed on some other private island. Listen, I'm not dismissing anything Talisa has been through. I know what it's like to be held against your will. But, umm, when Maya and Pretty Boy Mike had me, I was chained the fuck up in a dirty, grimy basement not some exotic island. The point is, I want you to stop blaming yourself."

"I appreciate you being here for me, Precious, and not looking at me like I'm this despicable person."

"Because you're not. I'm not only proud of you for coming clean with Genesis, but also for keeping yourself together. You're pregnant by the man you love and his long lost wife reappears after all these years and they're back together. I don't know many women who would be strong enough to handle that. Hell, I consider myself to be a bad bitch, but I might've gone ham by now."

"I seriously doubt it. You can pretty much get through anything, Precious."

"Maybe, but everyone has a breaking point. Have you spoken to Genesis since he brought Talisa home?"

"Nope. He's probably still angry with me."

"Well, he needs to get over it. You're the reason he has her back. Plus, you're carrying his child. That's something Genesis and Talisa will have to deal with. They might as well start now. That baby you're carrying..." Precious nodded at Skylar's stomach, "isn't going anywhere. You will forever be connected to Genesis and that's a fact. So all parties involved need to figure out how to make it work. My Goddaughter deserves that." Precious winked.

Skylar was soaking in everything that Precious said. She hated being the odd woman out, but she had to accept it was what it was. Having to sit on the sideline and watch Genesis have the life with Talisa that she always wanted to share with him would be a massive blow. But Skylar made the decision to have his child knowing the situation, so she had no choice but to put on her big girl panties and deal with it.

Astrid entered the condo in Center City West discreetly. She used her key to get inside and the caretaker she hired had just finished making lunch when she arrived.

"Good afternoon, Mrs. Bryant."

"Hello, Fatima. How's everything going?"

"Good. I just finished feeding Mr. Douglass and he's resting."

"Wonderful. You can go ahead and take a break. I'll stay here."

"Are you sure?"

"Positive. Take as long as you like."

"Thank you so much, Mrs. Bryant." Fatima beamed.

"My pleasure."

Fatima quickly grabbed her purse and keys and headed out to run a few errands with the unexpected free time she was getting. Astrid then went to the bedroom. Her brother was lying in bed watching television.

"How's my big brother doing today?"

Arnez turned and smiled when he saw his sister standing in the doorway. "Much better now that my beautiful sister is here. Come, sit down next to me." Arnez patted a space next to him on the bed.

"Every time I come, you're looking better and better."

"No, I don't. Between these burn marks and being confined to this bed, I look like shit. But at least I'm alive and that's all because of you." Arnez gave a slight grin.

Astrid hated seeing her brother like this, but he was in much better condition than when she found him barely clinging to life. With each visit he seemed to be getting stronger and healthier. After Supreme left him for dead, it wasn't looking good for Arnez. Luckily, Astrid had been coming to come see him once a week while he was recuperating in that house in upstate New York. Thank goodness for Arnez that his sister showed up when she did because if it had been one day later, he would've been a dead man.

Astrid made a call to a private doctor who was able to come over immediately and basically bring him back from being on the brink of death. Once he was well enough to travel, Astrid had Arnez brought to Philadelphia so she could watch over him while he got better.

"I hate to take that smile off your face, but there's something I need to tell you," Astrid said.

"What is it?"

"I know I haven't been over to see you for awhile, but so much has happened. Theron is dead, Fulton is dead, Genesis is out on bail, and Talisa is home with him. I know none of this is what you wanted to hear, but I promised that I would always tell you the truth no matter how awful it might be."

Arnez banged his fist on the bed and kept banging it over and over until she held his arms down.

"Stop it! You know that isn't good for your health. You're supposed to be getting better. You don't need a setback," she reminded Arnez.

"I want Talisa back! She can't be with Genesis. He doesn't deserve to be happy. He must suffer every day of his life."

"Relax. Genesis will be dealt with. You only have to focus on getting better so you can get out this bed. I'll take care of the rest. Starting with Genesis," Astrid promised.

"You always know the right thing to say," Arnez said, squeezing her hand. "I can trust that you will make sure my plan for Genesis is executed perfectly. With everyone thinking I'm dead they'll never see me coming."

Arnez was correct. He was not on anyone's

radar. Genesis did believe he had another enemy lurking in the shadows but Arnez had become irrelevant to him. Little did he know that his worst enemy was simply buying time and healing his body. Once he regained his strength, Arnez was coming for Genesis and he planned on taking his entire family with him.

P.O. Box 912
Collierville, TN 38027

A KING PRODUCTION

www.joydejaking.com
www.twitter.com/joydejaking

ORDER FORM

Name:

Address:

City/State:

Zip:

QUANTITY	TITLES	PRICE	TOTAL
	Bitch	$15.00	
	Bitch Reloaded	$15.00	
	The Bitch Is Back	$15.00	
	Queen Bitch	$15.00	
	Last Bitch Standing	$15.00	
	Superstar	$15.00	
	Ride Wit' Me	$12.00	
	Ride Wit' Me Part 2	$15.00	
	Stackin' Paper	$15.00	
	Trife Life To Lavish	$15.00	
	Trife Life To Lavish II	$15.00	
	Stackin' Paper II	$15.00	
	Rich or Famous	$15.00	
	Rich or Famous Part 2	$15.00	
	Rich or Famous Part 3	$15.00	
	Bitch A New Beginning	$15.00	
	Mafia Princess Part 1	$15.00	
	Mafia Princess Part 2	$15.00	
	Mafia Princess Part 3	$15.00	
	Mafia Princess Part 4	$15.00	
	Mafia Princess Part 5	$15.00	
	Boss Bitch	$15.00	
	Baller Bitches Vol. 1	$15.00	
	Baller Bitches Vol. 2	$15.00	
	Baller Bitches Vol. 3	$15.00	
	Bad Bitch	$15.00	
	Still The Baddest Bitch	$15.00	
	Power	$15.00	
	Power Part 2	$15.00	
	Drake	$15.00	
	Drake Part 2	$15.00	
	Female Hustler	$15.00	
	Female Hustler Part 2	$15.00	
	Female Hustler Part 3	$15.00	
	Female Hustler Part 4	$15.00	
	Female Hustler Part 5	$15.00	
	Female Hustler Part 6	$15.00	
	Princess Fever "Birthday Bash"	$6.00	
	Nico Carter The Men Of The Bitch Series	$15.00	
	Bitch The Beginning Of The End	$15.00	
	Supreme...Men Of The Bitch Series	$15.00	
	Bitch The Final Chapter	$15.00	
	Stackin' Paper III	$15.00	
	Men Of The Bitch Series And The Women Who Love Them	$15.00	
	Coke Like The 80s	$15.00	
	Baller Bitches The Reunion Vol. 4	$15.00	
	Stackin' Paper IV	$15.00	
	The Legacy	$15.00	
	Lovin' Thy Enemy	$15.00	
	Stackin' Paper V	$15.00	
	The Legacy Part 2	$15.00	
	Assassins - Episode 1	$11.00	
	Assassins - Episode 2	$11.00	
	Bitch Chronicles	$40.00	

Shipping/Handling (Via Priority Mail) $7.50 1-2 Books, $15.00 3-4 Books add $1.95 for ea. Additional book.
Total: $_____ FORMS OF ACCEPTED PAYMENTS: Certified or government issued checks and money Orders, all mail in orders take 5-7 Business days to be delivered

Made in the USA
Middletown, DE
27 July 2019